NECESSARY RISKS.

NECESSARY
RISKS

A Novel by Janet Keller

Turner Publishing, Inc.

ATLANTA

PUBLISHED BY TURNER PUBLISHING, INC.

A SUBSIDIARY OF TURNER BROADCASTING SYSTEM, INC.

ONE CNN CENTER, BOX 105366

ATLANTA, GEORGIA 30348-5366

FIRST EDITION 10 9 8 7 6 5 4 3 2 1

NECESSARY RISKS

KELLER, JANET

ISBN 1-878685-38-4

DISTRIBUTED BY ANDREWS AND MCMEEL

4900 MAIN STREET

KANSAS CITY, MISSOURI 64112

ALAN SCHWARTZ, EDITOR-IN-CHIEF

KATHERINE BUTTLER, ASSOCIATE EDITOR

MARIAN LORD, LYNN MCGILL, COPY EDITORS

CRAWFORD BARNETT, EDITORIAL ASSISTANT

MICHAEL WALSH, DESIGN DIRECTOR

KAREN SMITH, DESIGN/PRODUCTION

ELAINE STREITHOF, DESIGN/PRODUCTION

NANCY ROBINS, PRODUCTION DIRECTOR

ANNE MURDOCH, PRODUCTION COORDINATOR

Turner

I WISH TO EXPRESS my appreciation to the following writers:

Cathy Trost for *Elements of Risk: The Chemical Industry and Its Threat to America,*
Times Books, 1984.

Carol Van Strum for *A Bitter Fog: Herbicides and Human Rights,*
Sierra Club Books, 1983.

Dwight Holing for *California Wild Lands, a Guide to the Nature Conservancy Preserves,*
Chronicle Books, 1988.

ACKNOWLEDGMENTS

I AM DEEPLY GRATEFUL to the following for their support and encouragement: Alan Schwartz, Betty Ballantine, Andrew Goldblatt, and Penelope Moffet.

Special thanks to my father, Ormand Keller, and to my four sons —Troy, Ormand, Skyler, and William—and to the book's godmother, Cindy Garcia, who deserves special recognition for her generosity, wisdom, and perseverance.

C O N V E R G E N C E

"Lives converge for a reason."

TIMOTHY HARRIS

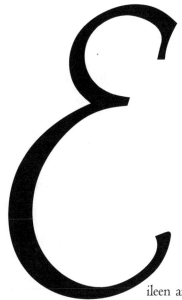ileen and I met the autumn of my junior year at UC Berkeley. If I'd been more stubborn when the time came for me to go away to college in the first place, we'd never have known each other.

The evening I told my Aunt Nell I'd changed my mind about going to Berkeley, that I'd decided to go to UCLA so I could keep my part-time job at the Los Angeles Zoo, she gave me a long look and said she didn't think that was a good idea.

We were seated at the old oak table in her dining room. Catalogues from colleges that had accepted me were spread out on the table. Nell picked up the one from Berkeley and riffled through it.

Her expression told me what she was thinking. The science program was one of the best preparatory courses in the country for veterinary school, and I'd already sent in my acceptance letter. Everything was in motion for me to go there. Also, since Berkeley was only an eight-hour drive from Nell's, I could spend holidays and vacations with her and continue working summers at the Los Angeles Zoo to help with my college expenses.

Finally Nell put down the catalogue. "We've talked about this, Nora."

I knew I was backpedaling, trying to change the parameters of my world as little as possible. But what was so terrible about that?

I said, "Think of the money we'll save if I keep on living here."

"There are other, more important things to consider. You need to get away."

"Not yet. I can do two years here, then transfer to Berkeley."

"It will be just as hard—if not harder—two years from now."

I glared at her. She knew what was troubling me. I didn't want to have to put it into words.

But she just waited.

"All right!" I said finally. "What if the same thing happens that happened in high school?"

"I don't believe it will, Nora. You've worked hard and you're stronger than you've ever been. It's time for you to come to terms with your past and future, and you can't do that staying home."

I didn't want to hear any more and ran out of the room.

But she was firm with me that summer—firmer than she'd been the whole thirteen years I'd lived with her.

So I went to Berkeley.

DURING THE EARLY PART of my freshman year, a 7.1 earthquake blacked out the entire city of San Francisco, cracked open a freeway approach to the Bay Bridge, and toppled several old buildings. Growing up in Santa Monica, I'd experienced a few quakes, but nothing like this one.

A feverish aura of excitement pervaded the campus for almost a month after the earthquake. Strangers smiled at one another. Normally stingy people joined in donating food and clothing to the needy. Panhandlers never had it so good. Students clustered in conversational groups on steps of buildings and in halls and libraries and gathered at night in the cafés until I wondered if that was the kind of atmosphere that had pervaded Berkeley when my parents were there in the late sixties. My mother had been an ardent advocate of the Free Speech movement. My father was among the first group of young men granted conscientious-objector status on nonreligious grounds during the Vietnam War, and he'd done his "tour of duty" working as an orderly in a VA hospital.

But by the end of my first semester, I'd forgotten all about the quake and its strange aftermath, and I'd also just about stopped worrying about running into my parents' ghosts. The things they'd believed in had disappeared. Rockridge, the impoverished neighborhood where they'd lived, had become a yuppie haven for trendy pizza and croissant parlors. People's Park, where my mother had been arrested by the National Guard, was a hangout for druggies and the destitute. Every time city hall threatened to turn the place into a parking lot or volleyball courts, homeless people staged protest sit-ins, but the students paid little attention. Sproul Plaza, where my father had given impassioned speeches encouraging draft resistance, was just a square students walked through on their way to class. An occasional demonstration there against injustice somewhere set off some sparks—but they quickly died. During my sophomore year when the Gulf War broke out, a few candlelight demonstrations were held on campus, and that was it. So there were no ghosts, nothing to interfere with my progress toward veterinary school. In fact, with the student-professor ratio at 100 to 1 in undergrad lecture classes and with tired, indifferent teaching assistants, my courses were easy.

But I knew things were supposed to get tougher in upper division classes, so at the beginning of my junior year, I decided to try and escape my overcrowded dorm and look for an affordable apartment.

I certainly wasn't optimistic about finding one. Apartments in Berkeley were scarce at the start of a school year, and having worked at my summer job in Los Angeles right up to the week classes started, I hadn't allowed myself much looking time. As I anticipated, the first places I called about had been rented. Relinquishing hope of total privacy, I turned to the "Roommate Wanted" columns. Again, the first few were taken. But my fifth call was answered by a woman who gave me an address on Benvenue—a street I'd walked down enough times to remember its charming old houses converted into apartments and duplexes. If there was a vacancy on that street at the rent I could afford, it had to be a closet.

The house turned out to be a tall, narrow mustard-colored Victorian, its windows framed by dark brown shutters. I tapped the brass knocker, and the door was opened by a woman in a wheelchair. Her short dark hair had a coppery glint, and her hazel eyes seemed large—perhaps because they were so animated. It was difficult to tell, but I thought she was several years older than I, maybe in her late twenties.

She also sized me up.

"Nora Holing?"

I nodded.

"I'm Eileen Mallory. Come in." Her quick handshake was strong.

She wheeled away from the open door and down an entry hall to a living room with high beamed ceilings, oak floors, and a bay window overlooking a narrow overgrown yard. An archway on the left opened onto a dining room with lovely old wainscoting.

Pointing to a door to my right, Eileen said, "The bedrooms are through there. Mine is the front one. Go and have a look at the back one, unless—"

I was already halfway across the living room. I turned. "Unless?"

"Nothing. Apparently the wheelchair doesn't bother you."

I blushed, not knowing why exactly. It was a trait Nell said I'd inherited from my mother, whose emotions often affected her complexion.

Eileen went on, "Actually, I get around on walking sticks most of the time, but not always, so I like prospective roommates to see me in the chair. Saves time and trouble in the long run."

I waited to see whether she was finished. When she didn't say anything more, I asked, "Can I look at the room now?"

She nodded, the trace of a smile flickering at the corners of her mouth.

The door opened onto a hallway leading past two bedrooms and a bathroom in between. The back bedroom was freshly painted. It had two windows—one looking out at the overgrown yard, the other onto a crimson bougainvillea sprawling over a gray slat fence. A bureau and bed frame had been pushed against one wall next to an old over-stuffed chair. The corner between the windows was empty, and I could picture my desk there.

When I went back to the living room, the wheelchair was parked near a wall. Eileen, on walking sticks, was standing near the fireplace. "Well?"

"It's lovely," I said, aware of the question my voice held.

"But?"

"Why is the rent so low?"

Moving to a couch near the fireplace, Eileen transferred the walking stick in her left hand to her right, braced herself with the two sticks in her right hand, and reaching behind with her left, sat down. It was laborious to watch and I could only imagine what it must be like to do it.

Propping the walking sticks against the couch arm, she said, "Three years ago, when I was twenty-seven, I started to trip and drop things. My doctor was puzzled until later I developed a blurred spot in one eye—the requisite symptom for him to be able to make a diagnosis: Multiple Sclerosis."

She paused then and looked up.

I sat down facing her.

"Would you like some coffee or tea?"

I shook my head.

"If you did, I'd tell you to go in the kitchen and help yourself. Like Scarecrow in Oz, I lose a lot of my stuffing during the course of a day, so I'm frequently bitchy. I can blame some of that on being a second-year law student, but MS is the real culprit. On bad days, I need help with things like opening jars, turning faucets, pulling up zippers, sometimes even getting on and off the toilet. Which is part of the answer to your question about the rent."

"I understand," I said.

"Really? What do you do, take care of invalids in a nursing home?"

"Summers I work with animals at the Los Angeles Zoo. Newborns and sick ones often need help."

"Why do you have that job?"

"What?"

"Do you have some kind of do-good complex?"

"It helps pays the bills and it's related to what I want to be—a veterinarian."

"How did you decide on that?"

"I love animals."

"Human ones included?"

I lied a little. "A few."

Her interrogation had been so intense, I felt relieved when she eased up. That trace of a smile touched her lips again then faded. "I have a short MS lecture I give prospective roommates, but I might as well say a dozen people before you looked at the apartment. Half walked out on the toilet seat line. The rest left after the lecture. I just want you to know you don't have to be polite and sit through it. You're free to go."

Her eyes were challenging me, yet something in their expression also made me want to stay. And from a selfish point of view, the house was peaceful and quiet. So I said, "I always stick around for the first five minutes of any lecture. That way I can make up my own mind whether I'm going to learn anything."

She raised an eyebrow, and I thought she might say something unrehearsed. But a second later, she started. "Multiple Sclerosis is a chronic degenerative disease of the central nervous system. Picture corroded telephone wires, and you'll be close. Victims can lose vision, hearing, speech, the ability to walk, practically everything, including coordination.

"Sudden debilitating attacks called exacerbations can happen, but I haven't had any. Since my MS stabilized two years ago, my biggest problem has been spastic legs, and a compelling need when I'm in unfamiliar surroundings to know where the bathroom is."

"Well, I like knowing that myself," I murmured, hoping to help her relax a little.

Without giving any sign she'd heard me, she went on, "Last item: I *hate* having MS. Finding ways to ignore or ridicule it is my best defense. But it retaliates by knocking me flat with fatigue—which I resist until some part of me breaks down. And that's also where my roommate comes in. I have a specially equipped Toyota van, and days when my legs are behaving like addicts in need of a fix, it helps if the person who lives with me will act as chauffeur."

"I don't see any problem with that."

"What do you see a problem with?"

"Not being able to rent the room."

She smiled for the first time. "So you're willing to take on a monster who twitches and bitches?"

I shrugged. "You couldn't be worse than a panther with the flu."

MY FIRST FEW WEEKS with Eileen were exhausting. The expression in her hazel eyes was often defiant, and her posture even in the wheelchair was aggressive. I'd never lived with a person who needed me like that. Watching her struggle with some task, knowing she could verbalize what she wanted, I couldn't guess when I should offer assistance. It was maddening.

One evening, as I studied at the dining room table, my concentration was interrupted by her struggle with the electric can opener in the kitchen. Suddenly an unopened can came flying through the doorway, hitting the old wainscoting.

I jumped up. "What was *that* for?"

She was at the doorway by then and in a fury. "Why don't you ever offer help?"

"Why don't you tell me when you need it?"

"You're supposed to know!"

"How? ESP?"

Our mutual rage cleared the air a little bit, and after that, I tried harder and so did she—but our timing was still ragged.

About a week after the can opener incident, Eileen lost a wrestling match with a ketchup bottle; it slipped out of her fingers and smashed in the kitchen sink. Trying to clean it up, she cut herself. While I was bandaging her finger, our eyes met. She looked away quickly, but not before I'd seen her anguish. That haunted me, and for a while my offers of help verged on the intrusive, which had the effect of making her tell me more often when she needed help. So brick by brick, the walls did begin to come down.

Then I had to confront the possibility I might actually like this woman, and that scared me because ever since my parents died the only person I'd risked caring about was my Aunt Nell.

Maybe I was drawn to Eileen because she was bright and unpredictable. Or maybe because coping with MS forced her to show me her darkness, and I was beginning to wish I could show someone mine.

When I was about ten years old, I put a picture of my parents on the nightstand next to my bed because it seemed important to remember what they looked like, and I also wanted to understand the ways I resembled them. Nell said, "You have your mother's complexion and hair color and her height and quick way of moving. But your face is very like your father's." In the photograph, my father had long dark hair, a beard, and wore glasses that magnified his eyes. His eyes were brooding, but his mouth looked as if it could smile easily. My mother's hair was the same wheat color as mine, and I suspected she had freckles like mine, too, only the photograph didn't show them. Both my parents gazed thoughtfully at the camera, their hands clasped.

I don't know why I chose that particular picture. Nell had others, as well as several taken of her and my father when they were children. Even though Nell was five years older than my father, she said they'd never had a typical older sister–younger brother relationship. They'd simply liked one another. A lot.

So she'd put all the pictures in an album, together with a few mementoes, saying the album would be mine when I cared to claim it. I knew this was part of her endeavor to help me understand my parents' lives, but I couldn't. It seemed to me their whole existence had led up to dying young. On May 4, 1977, they were driving their Volkswagen "Bug" back from New Hampshire, where they'd participated in a demonstration against the construction of the Seabrook nuclear plant.

On an old country highway, one of their tires blew; they careened off the road into a telephone pole. Before rescuers could get them out, the rust-riddled fuel tank exploded and the car went up in flames.

Nell always said, "It was the stupidest kind of accident."

I thought it was stupid, too—but not the way Nell did. If they'd been different kinds of people, they would have been driving a different car. Or they would have taken better care of the one they had. Or they wouldn't have gone to New Hampshire in the first place.

I was seven years old when I went to live with Nell, who became my guardian and brought me to her house in Santa Monica. She completely accepted me so that I grew to love and trust her. Also, her life made sense to me; it was sane and reasonable. She seemed invincible.

Eileen was just the opposite.

BY THE END OF THE FIRST month, we'd gotten in the habit of sharing the living room in the evenings while we studied. Increasingly aware of the volume of work she had to do, I was curious why she'd chosen law.

One chilly night, after we'd spent several silent hours immersed in our books and the fire I'd built had dwindled to embers, I just came right out and asked her—why law?

She shook her head. "I doubt anybody can understand that, except me. My parents certainly don't."

"What do you mean?"

"At the time I got MS, I was an account executive at a public relations firm in Boston. I'd worked hard to get that position, and the management held it open for me. But by the time my MS stabilized, I didn't give a shit about public relations. Having been attacked by a virus nobody knows how to do anything about—'a bum rap,' as my Uncle Willis would say—to keep from going crazy, or worse, turning into a martyr, I had to find some way to use my anger to accomplish something. Getting a black belt in karate was the first thing that came to mind, but that stage soon passed. After a lot of thought and investigation, working toward a law degree made sense to me. I applied to several law schools and thanks to high LSAT scores and admission mandates for women and the handicapped, I was provisionally accepted here at Boalt."

" 'Provisionally'?"

"Meaning I have to paddle my oar hard enough to maintain a 'B' average, which, so far, I've managed to do."

She looked at me. "Any comment?"

"What about?"

"Somebody with MS wanting to be a lawyer."

"No."

"You think it's possible?"

"Depends on the person."

"Yeah? I wish my parents believed that. They think I'm out of my mind." She started stacking her law books. "How do yours feel about what you're doing?"

"My parents are dead," I said flatly.

She gave me a startled look. "I'm sorry."

I didn't say anything for a minute. Then: "Actually, they got what . . ." but I didn't finish the sentence and for a fleeting moment, their ghosts were there. Abruptly I stood up and stirred the remains of the fire, staring intently at the flickering remains.

"Nora?"

I turned.

"Sometimes it helps to talk about it."

Lamplight accentuated the shadows under her eyes, marking her fatigue, and for some reason, that, too, made me think of them.

The next thing I knew, I was telling her about my parents—the things they'd done in the sixties and seventies, the way they died; how as a child, I sensed they loved me, but their attention was always on things that were so much bigger that I couldn't ever seem to make them see me. Having come that far, I told her about Nell and my stormy adolescence, when my unresolved rage and grief had finally imploded into a dangerous depression. I'd gotten incompletes in all my courses because I stopped going to high school. Then I wouldn't leave my room for meals. The few friends I had stopped calling. I avoided everything. I slept or read or stared at the tree outside my window.

"How did you get out of that?" Eileen asked softly.

"Nell," I said.

"What did she do?"

"Normally, she works in a studio behind her house drawing illustrations for children's books. During my breakdown, she set up an easel in my room and did her illustrations there." I smiled at the memory, remembering how her plain almost stern face always seemed lit from within by her absorption in her work.

"Because she was right in front of me, I started watching her draw. She'd explain how she used shading to create mood, or accentuated a feature to reveal personality. Sometimes she'd ask my opinion about color. I began to understand the comfort work could bring and to wish I had something to do, too.

"Gradually, I became able to leave my room. In the beginning, it was just into the hall, then downstairs, then outside while Nell watered the rose bushes. One day she persuaded me to go with her to the zoo. While she sat drawing, I wandered around among the enclosures, staring in at the birds, animals, and reptiles, who, in turn, gazed right back at me and seemed interested in who I was. Soon, I actually looked forward to those trips to the zoo. Nell could spend most of a day sketching. And the hours I spent observing the animals brought out a deep love for them. After I got a job at the zoo, helping with newborn and sick animals, I'm not sure who depended on whom more. I decided I wanted to become a veterinarian and once I'd settled on that goal, it turned into a road back, and I was able to function fairly well in the 'normal' world—as long as people left me alone."

After I'd finished, my throat felt as if it were lined with sawdust. I also wondered if I'd revealed too much.

"Well, except for times when somebody like me sticks her nose in your business, you seem okay. You seem fine," Eileen said.

"I do, huh?"

"The thing is," she continued softly, "you have to let the world in sometimes if only because it's bigger than you are."

Her words brought up an issue already putting out tiny thorns between us: She'd recently volunteered twenty hours a week at the Bay Area Community Law Center where second-year law students were trained to handle routine trial work for the homeless and disabled. I'd asked her how she expected to find time to do that and still get all her studying done. She'd just said, "I'll work it out."

Looking at her now, curled up on the sofa, a law book on her lap, her walking sticks propped up against the sofa back, I asked myself, How could I possibly risk caring about someone already in so much jeopardy?

AS THE WEEKS PASSED and our friendship deepened, I became aware of the strict measures Eileen used to maintain what she called her "margin of safety" with her disease. Hoping to increase the amount of stress she could handle, she kept records of her symptoms and was careful of foods that might aggravate them. Chocolate was a demon for her, yet she craved it—especially when she stayed up studying after midnight. "*Gawd*," she would complain, "if only tort law were *chocolate* torte, I could polish it off in twenty seconds!"

To save her sanity, she occasionally went out on what she called "slapstick dates," usually with a member of her study group. If there was a Laurel and Hardy or Chaplin or Buster Keaton movie playing, they would see it.

I didn't date in those days, but was curious about what it might be like—to be with someone, to make love, or even to want to make love.

During one of our after-midnight gabfests—we'd polished off a bottle of wine at about two o'clock in the morning—I asked Eileen if she made love with any of the men she dated.

She gave me a look. "Are you kidding? No second-year law student has time for sex." Then more seriously, "I wouldn't be able to handle somebody else's uncertainty plus my own. If I ever met someone who wasn't embarrassed, who could laugh with me . . . well, never mind."

The wine allowed me to persist. "So, are you a virgin?"

"No. I had a few affairs before I got MS—which I'm glad about now. Jesus, can you imagine being a virgin with MS!" She stared into her glass. "I even thought I was in love once. And then I found out I wasn't. One thing about this disease—it can be a great clarifier."

The sudden strain in her voice let me know I shouldn't pursue that topic further.

We both were hanging on tenterhooks anyway about the outcome of mid-term exams. I was finding out the work really was harder in upper level classes. And I was positive Eileen spent too much time at that damned Community Law Center. The phone rang a lot more often than it had when I first moved in. And because the combination of being nervous and in a crowd caused her legs to go spastic, she'd had to make her first courtroom appearance on behalf of the Center in her wheelchair. "The last thing I need to do is fall down in front of the judge," she jibed.

As her workload increased, she asked me to drive her to the court-house a couple of times, which didn't bother me. What did, was her increasing tiredness. Sometimes at night when we settled down in the living room to study, she'd immediately fall asleep and the next day would have to trust to luck she wouldn't be called on.

It didn't make sense to me, especially when I knew how badly she wanted to be chosen to work on the law review her last year. Despite the long hours that would entail, at least there was a point to it; working on the review would improve her chances of being hired by one of the public-interest law firms she was interested in.

One day when she had not one but two courtroom appearances for the Center, I drove her to the courthouse in the morning and picked her up in the afternoon. She'd been there over five hours. She leaned tiredly on her walking sticks as I was folding her wheelchair to load it in the back of the van. Suddenly I was angry. "How much longer do you think you can go on juggling law school, your work for the Center, *and* your health?"

"As long as I have to."

I shook my head.

"Damn it, Nora, people's willingness to confront moral issues ebbs and flows. Right now we're in an ebb cycle. The number of people living on the street increases every year. Students eat their lunch in cafés, then step around the homeless on their way to class. Those people are victims just like me. And I can help them."

"At what cost?"

She gave me a baffled look. "The only 'cost' would come from not trying to help."

The ride home was silent.

ABOUT HALFWAY INTO THE semester, I noticed Eileen's "slapstick dates" narrowing down to two people, Bill-something-or-other from her study group and Rupert Hawkins, whom she'd met at the Center. Rupert was black and brilliant and didn't ever let anybody forget either one. He had a high forehead and a jutting jaw, which he enjoyed thrusting at people. But his gray-green eyes were his most arresting feature. If he caught somebody sneaking a look at him— which happened often because his eyes were so startling against his brown skin—he'd smile slyly and murmur, "Well, my great grand-pappy, old Tom Jefferson, you know, he was a green-eyed devil." Which Eileen thought was funny, and I thought was overbearing.

As it turned out, Rupert's involvement at the Center was short-lived. The day he completed his training, he announced he was only going to work on cases involving equal housing and employment opportunities for blacks. When the head of the Center told him he'd have to accept cases including non-blacks as well, Rupert walked out.

Eileen tried hard to convince him to change his mind, arguing that injustice affected all human beings.

"You could say that," Rupert agreed. "Or you could say some slack needs taking up since blacks have been denied fair representation in the American court system for over two centuries."

For a while, their debate interested me, especially after Rupert told Eileen over dinner at our house one evening, "Baby, your idealism is useless. Just don't delude yourself into believing anything you do will last."

Another evening he quoted one of his idols, Florynce Kennedy, a black lawyer during the sixties and seventies. "Old Flo, she said, 'Go to the ghetto, listen to the people. But don't stay too long, and for Christ's sake, don't get in bed with the patient. If you want to kill poverty, go to Wall Street and kick ass.' "

Eileen remarked she'd been on the equivalent of Wall Street at the public relations firm in Boston, and didn't think it was a great place to work miracles.

But after a while I began to wish they'd put their argument to rest. One evening when I had a difficult paper to write, I stomped down the hallway and told them to go argue in Rupert's apartment.

His smile was wicked. "Can't do that, Nora. My roommates are studying."

I took the bait. "Well, so am I . . . and Eileen should be, too! If you gave a damn, you'd understand she has enough to cope with without trying to straighten you out."

I'd scored. I could see it in his eyes. But before either of us could position new arrows, Eileen exploded. "Shit! Don't ever intercede for me, Nora! I don't need it and I don't want it."

I was so hurt and furious that if Rupert had been a foot closer I would have kicked him. Later I wished I had because what I did was worse. I ordered them to take their argument out into the street or to a bar. "And if you're not willing to do that, I'll be happy to move out and Rupert can move in. A chauffeur's cap would look better on him than me anyway."

It was a horrible thing to say.

I turned around and went back down the hallway to my room. A few minutes later, I heard Rupert leave. Eileen went to her room. Then silence.

I lay awake for hours asking myself, What had really been going on with me? With Rupert? It went deeper than my being annoyed by the sound of their arguing. Everything about him was intrusive. And then I saw it. He loved her just as I did. He was afraid for her just as I was. And I'd used my concern for her to cover up something I didn't want to look at: jealousy of the time she spent with him. Understanding that didn't make me like him any better, but at least I could acknowledge how ashamed I felt about the way I'd acted.

The next morning I apologized to Eileen. I told her I was sorry for the way I'd behaved and murmured that when I saw Rupert, I'd try to make amends.

Looking at me with the same close scrutiny she had the day we met, Eileen said, "You have your rights, too, Nora."

I did apologize to Rupert the next time he came to the house, and it wasn't easy. He had his shields up. Knowing whatever I said would just bounce off, I said woodenly, "I'm sorry about the other night," and continued on out the door. But I felt those eyes boring into my back. After that, he spent as little time as possible at the house when I was there. He would come as far as the entry hall when he picked Eileen up and fidget until she was ready to leave.

Eileen and I lived in a guarded state of truce until one afternoon in March when she came home early. Dropping her law books on the sofa, she announced, "We have to talk."

"Okay."

"I'm not going to have any casework at the Center for a couple of weeks."

"That's great. How come?"

She explained that the Center, always underfunded, had been offered a challenge grant. If they could raise $25,000 in private donations, a San Francisco foundation would match that amount. Because of her public relations background, she'd been asked to run the fundraising drive.

"Meaning?" I asked warily.

"For the next few weeks, some other people from the Center and I are going to put out a massive mailing—to Bay Area law firms, corporations, anybody we can think of who might part with some money."

"Uh-huh."

Her eyes held mine. "The thing is, the Center is really cramped for space. We're going to move the copy machine and computer over here and use the living room."

"Here? Our living room?"

"Yes."

I just stared at her.

"Look, it's only for three or four weeks. You don't have to be involved. You're in lab afternoons. If you shut the door to your room in the evenings, you probably won't even hear us. And there's always the library."

"When do you plan to study?"

"When I can. I'll make time. This is important."

"So is getting your law degree," I snapped. "How can you do that if you're running a fund-raising drive?"

"It's only a short while, Nora." She was trembling, which often happened when she was upset. "The Center needs this money."

"I don't give a goddamn what the Center needs. I need peace and quiet! And so do you."

The look on her face was worse than any words.

"Why are you looking at me like that?"

"You can't go on ignoring things because they don't immediately affect you. Some day they're going to. Damn it, your parents were working to change things. They—"

"Died trying!" I shot back, cutting her off. The rest of what I wanted to say—"And so will you!"—clogged in my throat.

But maybe she heard it anyway.

We reimposed the ban of silence on social issues after that. Afternoons, I stayed in lab as late as I could, and Eileen and the people from the Center used the living room freely. In the evenings, I could tell they were trying hard to keep their voices down.

But the atmosphere between Eileen and me was strained.

It didn't make me feel better when I discovered Rupert agreed with me. Eileen stopped seeing him or anybody else except the fund-raising group, but I ran into him on campus one afternoon. We gave each other curt nods, and I thought that was going to be it; but when he was almost past me, he stopped, turned around, and started walking alongside me. "She's been having a hard time in class. How come you're letting her do that shit?" he demanded.

"I'm not her keeper."

"Thought you were, that it went with the chauffeur's cap."

"Fuck you."

"In your dreams, baby," he said and walked away.

Two-and-a-half weeks later the mailings were finished. Thanks to generous donations from several law firms, the drive was successful.

Eileen and I gave each other a wide berth for a while, but eventually things returned to our version of normal.

ON A CHILLY APRIL AFTERNOON when winds from the Pacific Northwest were blowing through Berkeley, I went into a small cafeteria near campus for some soup. A lot of other people had the same idea. I saw a few empty seats but no unoccupied tables. Standing in the middle of the room holding my tray, I noticed a young man seated alone at a table for two; he was eating his soup while reading a textbook and taking notes. The fluorescent ceiling light accentuated a small bald spot on top of his head and the fringe of blond hair around it that looked like a collapsed halo. He seemed a studious type who wouldn't attempt conversation; besides, my soup was getting cold.

He must have sensed me watching him because he looked up and immediately nodded at the empty chair. While I was putting my tray on the table, my biology book slipped to the floor. He stood up to retrieve it and I saw how very thin and tall he was—probably around six-foot-three, and I doubt he weighed 170 pounds. Handing me the book, he asked which professor I had. It turned out he'd had the same one the previous year. Then he said his name was Timothy Harris and that he was a botany major.

"Nora Holing," I murmured.

"As in not 'halving', but 'Wholing'?"

"No. As in 'holing' up for the winter."

He closed his book and notebook and put them on the backpack beneath his chair. I thought he was getting ready to leave, but instead he smiled at me.

I smiled back.

"Do you have to study?" he asked.

"Always." But I didn't reach for my book.

Then he told me a story about the biology professor that made me laugh.

Something about him drew me out. Maybe it was the friendly, accepting expression in his brown eyes; or maybe because for me, it was time—past time.

I assumed he was older than I, perhaps because he looked like a graduate student, and was at ease with himself. I was startled to find out he was a junior like me—and a year younger. He said he'd skipped two grades in elementary school, ". . . probably because I spent ninety-nine percent of my time fiddling around with plants, and my teachers didn't know what else to do with me. Right now I live in the basement of my botany professor's house and earn my rent by taking care of her plants."

Then he asked if I'd like to come and meet his charges on Saturday afternoon.

I surprised myself by saying, "Yes."

That night, after Eileen and I settled down in the living room to study, I kept wriggling in my chair and reading the same page over. Finally, I shut my book. "Eileen."

She looked up. "Hm?"

"I met this guy today."

She grinned. "That's the most ordinary thing I've ever heard you say . . . 'I met this guy.' "

"Well, that's what happened."

"So tell me about him."

I did—though there wasn't much to tell.

When I'd finished, she nodded. "He sounds fine."

"Yeah. It's just . . ." I sighed. "I don't know."

She pushed her glasses down to the end of her nose and looked at me. "It's a little like skiing."

" 'Skiing'?"

"Uh-huh. The first time you put on skis, your body seems weird. It won't do anything you want it to. But you keep trying and trying and eventually everything falls into place, and you start getting those beautiful downhill runs and the world turns into a white Eden. Beginning a relationship, your feelings swerve and swoop out from under you. But after a while things settle down and it's like . . . the opposite of loneliness."

She had such a look of longing in her eyes, and I didn't know whether it was because she was remembering being able to ski or loving someone or both.

DESPITE MY SEVERE CASE of nerves, Berkeley had never seemed so beautiful to me as it did on Saturday. The sky was that teal-tinted blue that happens in northern California in the spring, and the breeze off the bay was cool and crisp. Everything I looked at seemed to be sparkling.

The house where Timothy lived was a two-mile walk from Eileen's and mine. A short flight of steps led down to his door. He opened it as soon as I knocked and invited me into a small basement apartment full of plants. They were everywhere—hanging from the ceiling, sitting on wooden boxes containing his music collection, perching on windowsills and bookshelves. He gave me a "tour," telling me a botanist, like a parent, couldn't have favorites. But one was special, the Santa Cruz Island Live-Forever he'd found on a botanical field trip to the island. The delicate succulent—the most fragile-looking I'd ever seen—sat on an orange crate next to his bed.

He put some CDs on his player, some water for tea on his hot plate, and we talked. For hours.

He was attending Berkeley on a Science Endowment Fellowship. His tuition and expenses were being paid in exchange for his working summers on SEF projects, and at the end of his senior year, the fellowship would continue at Harvard where he would start on his Ph.D.

"I'm a botany major because it's in the blood," he grinned. "My parents own a nursery in Boulder, Colorado, and my earliest memories are of being with them in the potting shed, touching and smelling earth, flowers, roots. I'm their only child and they were in their mid-forties when they had me, which is probably why I'm peculiar. Now, what about you?"

I told him about Nell and my dream of being a veterinarian in a small town and, more easily than I ever had anyone, about my parents. Though when I'd finished, that graininess was in my throat.

He touched my hand. "Parents are supposed to be our 'safe place,' " he said, "especially when we're young. If we lose them, we've lost part of ourselves."

I swallowed and nodded, having, as always, a tough time with sympathy.

"Listen," Timothy said, "a lot of plants out back are going to have hurt feelings if they don't get to meet you. Follow me."

He led the way to the professor's greenhouse and introduced me to his charges. Watching him gently stroke a tree-perching orchid from Java, I decided his hands were the most beautiful I'd ever seen. The fingers were long and tapering with tiny patches of pale blond hair just below the knuckle that made me want to reach out.

He said, "Flowers, like people, emit a seductive odor when they're ready to mate, and even have small attacks of fever."

Walking me home that evening, he asked matter-of-factly if I'd ever made love. I said, "No." Then he invited me to go across the Bay and visit the San Francisco Zoo the next weekend.

My concentration on my studies was web-thin that week as thoughts of Timothy turned the minutes into hours. Eileen thought I might be coming down with something, which I was.

Sunday rolled in foggy and chilly, so Timothy and I used that as an excuse to stay in. I think we would have even if it had been ninety degrees out, we both wanted so much to make love.

He lit two tall candles, placed them on the orange crate next to his bed and we took off our clothes while oval-shaped fog-drops slid down the windows.

I don't know what I expected love-making to be like. Nell had told me all the basic facts, and I'd read the textbook things and paid close attention to steamy love scenes in movies. But watching was one thing, participating another. I knew condoms existed, but I'd never seen one. Nor did I know that because I was a virgin, Timothy would have to struggle. When he came the first time without penetrating me, he swung around and sat on the edge of the bed, put his elbows on his knees and held his head in his hands.

"I'm sorry, Nora," he murmured.

I wasn't sure what the apology was for. Then he told me he'd never made love either. I pulled him back down beside me and we just held each other. After a while, he started touching me the same way he'd touched the orchid—lightly running his fingers over my skin, telling me softly I'd reminded him of a heron poised for flight in the café that day, and that was the name he was going to call me from now on. Then we were trying again, and this time I did my best to help. When my hymen broke, I was so astonished at the brief moment of small tearing pain, I said, "Oh!" And at that moment, Timothy came again. He whispered, "Heron," and I held him close until the trembling stopped. In the flickering light, his long thin body seemed much more lunar than earthly to me.

Hours later, as I was leaving, he gave me a book of poetry by Theodore Roethke. He said Roethke had grown up with plants, too, and had the gift of putting his feelings about them into words.

We saw each other almost every day after that, sometimes at his apartment, sometimes at the Benvenue house. We quickly got better at making love. I began to wonder how I'd ever existed without such sweetness in my life. He loved my long thin body and moody eyes and accepted everything about me—my constant nagging concern about Eileen; my determination to be a veterinarian in a small town where people lived uncomplicated, unthreatened lives; my confused feelings about my parents, and my avoidance of social issues.

As our relationship deepened and we spent more and more time together, Eileen made droll comments about our "third tenant," but it was obvious she and Timothy liked one another.

He, too, became concerned about what he called her "white heat intensity," and one evening when the shadows under her eyes were obvious, I heard him tell her, "When plants put out excess energy, there's always payback time."

"Don't confuse me with a rhododendron," she said and changed the subject.

The three of us started taking turns cooking dinner for each other on Sunday nights. Once in a while, Rupert joined us, and it turned out he knew how to do amazing things with vegetables. He also brought CDs of rock groups I'd never even heard of. Sometimes we danced, and watching Rupert with Eileen, observing the gentle, supportive way he held her almost made me forget how much I disliked him. Then he'd grab me for a wicked reggae number, showing off, and by the time it was over, I'd be ready to sock him.

Once in a while, I'd see Eileen studying Timothy with an expression I couldn't decipher. A couple of times when she'd been watching him and her eyes met mine, I sensed she didn't want me to decipher her thoughts.

I asked her about this one Sunday night after Timothy and Rupert had left.

"It's nothing."

"With you, it's never 'nothing.' "

"I've just been wondering . . ."

"What?"

"I've heard Timothy speak a lot about ecology and endangered species. He's about the most environmentally committed person I've ever met, out to save as much of the world as he can. I just wondered . . ."

"What?"

"How you felt about that?"

I hadn't felt anything. A jet of anger welled up. "I haven't analyzed my feelings about his commitment to the environment! Is there some law that says I have to? Can't I just love him?"

"I don't know. Can you?" she asked.

IN JUNE, I MOVED BACK into my room at Nell's house as I had every college summer and went to work at the Los Angeles Zoo to save up money for the fall.

Timothy was sent to an isolated agricultural research station in the San Joaquin Valley where plant breeders were trying to save some of the wild plants that had become nearly extinct when farmers turned forests into fields. He was out from dawn to dusk. Telephones were difficult for him to get to, but he wrote often telling me about his work. He was concerned about the loss of thousands of acres of ancestral grasses to irrigated fields in that valley. It also worried him that farmers in countries all over the world were growing the same sturdy, high-yield, drought-resistant wheat, because then everybody's wheat became vulnerable to the same viral or bacterial or insect foe. He said, "It's like putting the identical combination of numbers on bank vaults everywhere. One burglar could ransack them all."

On one of his rare afternoons off, he drove to the coast to see the redwoods in the old-growth forests, so many of which had been decimated. He wrote, "Heron, there are redwoods here over fifteen hundred years old. They were infants when Hannibal was leading his elephants over the Alps; they were two-hundred-year-old children when Jesus was born. In a way, they're still like children because they need protecting."

Eileen stayed alone in the Benvenue house, having made arrangements for a neighbor to come in and help. The Center went on half-day status during the summer, so she was able to spend long hours in the law library shoring herself up for her last year and filling out interview applications for clerkships. We talked frequently, and one evening in late July she called to tell me she hadn't been chosen for the law review so she was going to increase her commitment at the Center to twenty-five hours a week. From the tone in her voice, I even think she preferred it that way.

By the time I returned in late August, her work for the Center was already piling up, and I decided it would be better all around if, instead of grumbling and sulking, I pitched in to help her type briefs and letters.

"Great, Nora," she said with a grin. "Does that mean you've decided to join us in the human race?"

"Not the whole race," I said drily. "Maybe just a ten-mile run."

THE DAYS OF OUR LAST YEAR at Berkeley passed swiftly. Too swiftly.

Timothy, Eileen, and I quickly resumed our Sunday evening meal-sharing, with Rupert becoming a regular. He and I were more tolerant of one another because he liked Timothy so much. He called him "the brother of the plant world" and gave him the name of a close friend to look up when Timothy arrived at Harvard.

That October, Eileen received a letter from the U.S. Circuit Court of Appeals in Washington, D.C., in reply to one of her applications. Her hands were shaking as she opened the envelope. Taking the letter out, she dropped it, picked it up, read it, held it out to me, and while

I was reading that a judge on the court had granted her an interview, she disappeared down the hallway.

Moments later, I found her sitting on her bed, holding two pillows, and crying—Eileen, who never cried. "It's stupid to be carrying on like this," she said, dabbing her eyes with the corner of a pillowcase. "It's just a damned interview."

But her bedroom light was often on late at night after that as she put in extra hours researching the judge. When she'd finished, she told me, "The man has a reputation for choosing bleeding-heart liberals to be his clerks so he can Brillo our brains. Or, as one of his ex-staff put it, 'sharpen our intellects for a more suitable engagement with The Law.' " Her tone was disparaging, but that was defensive. Regardless of the man's politics, I knew how badly she wanted that clerkship. When Rupert told her she was crazy, the man would peel her soul like a grape, she smiled and said, "Honey, you know I don't peel easy." The interview was scheduled to take place over the Christmas vacation.

We were all going home for the holidays. Eileen planned to spend Christmas with her parents in Boston, then fly on to Washington for her meeting with the judge.

On the Monday before Christmas, I saw Timothy off on the Greyhound bus that would take him to Boulder. Earlier that week he'd found out that while he was at Harvard, his work assignment would take him to the Persian Gulf. Three months out of each school year he'd be assisting a team of scientists monitoring the long-term environmental effects of the war. He knew he'd see some terrible conditions, but believed the opportunity to study them would be invaluable. And, as always, he wanted to help reclaim what could be saved.

The thought of his being so far away loomed like a prison sentence in my mind, and this short separation was a foreshadowing. The bus depot waiting room was grim and smoke-filled with tired-looking Christmas wreaths hanging above the ticket windows. It depressed me far more than was reasonable. When it was time for Timothy to board the bus, I held him so tightly the buttons on his jacket made an imprint on my cheek.

The next day, I left for Nell's and dropped Eileen off at the airport on my way. Her hard work the past several weeks had taken its toll. She'd lost weight, and her shoulders drooped with exhaustion. She even had a thick packet of notes to study on the plane.

I told her crossly that if she didn't take some time to relax, she was going to make herself ill before she ever got to the interview.

"Hey, I've called all the movie theaters in Boston so I know exactly what's playing where. I'm going on a three-day movie binge before I fly to Washington. If that doesn't help, nothing will." But when I left her in the passenger terminal, she was already taking the rubber band off her notecards.

I continued south, arriving at Nell's a little after midnight. The next morning we decorated the giant cactus in her living room with chili-pepper lights as we had every Christmas since I'd been living with her. She had invited a few close friends for dinner on Christmas Eve, and I was much more at ease than I'd been on such occasions in the past, which pleased her. After her guests left and we were doing the dishes, she said, "You're changing. I wish your parents could know you."

I stopped drying a pan and looked at her. I was taller than she was, but somehow I never felt taller. "Why?" I said. "I'm not doing anything they believed in."

She said, "You're working hard toward a worthwhile goal. They certainly believed in that." And she shook her head. "If you could only get past your feeling that they deserted you, Nora, you'd realize they were vulnerable, too."

ON OUR FIRST DAY BACK at Berkeley, Eileen told me her interview with the judge hadn't gone well. As she'd anticipated, he made it clear pro bono work wouldn't be compatible with a clerkship, and he further warned her he'd seen too many brilliant young advocates emasculated trying to mesh compassion and reason.

"Don't you love it? 'Emasculated.' I think he forgot he was talking to a woman, or maybe he figured my walking sticks make me sexless. I told him I *feel* a lot of things, and how I feel has quite a bit to do with how I *think*, and there must be some way to reconcile the two. He responded by saying the meeting was over, and that, as they say, was that."

I felt disappointed for her, yet also was aware of a guilty sense of relief. If she didn't get a clerkship, maybe she'd stay on the West Coast.

But in the middle of March I heard from the veterinary school at UC Davis that I hadn't made the first round of acceptees. I'd been so confident that I hadn't applied to any other schools, and I was furious at myself. The letter did say I was on the list of alternates should anyone drop out. Fat chance of that, I thought, crumpling the piece of paper and throwing it across the room.

Eileen retrieved the letter, read it, and said, "Listen, I'm planning to open up a storefront law office in downtown Oakland. Why don't you set up shop next door? We can share a lease, and while I'm interviewing clients, you can treat their pets."

I glared at her and she started giggling. "Can't you just see it? 'Eileen Mallory, Rights Advocate for the Homeless,' and 'Nora Holing, Pro Bono Veterinarian.'"

A second later, helpless, I was laughing, too.

ONE MORNING THE telephone in the Benvenue house rang a little before seven. I was awake, but huddling in my warm blankets. In the kitchen, Eileen picked up the receiver, and I lay listening to the soft murmur of her voice until she yelped, "Nora!" Then I leapt up and ran down the hall, thinking she needed help.

She was sitting on one of the kitchen chairs. In the gray early light, her face was bright pink. Looking at me with a beatific smile, she said, "I got it."

"What?"

"That was Washington, the judge's secretary. He wants me, Nora. God, he wants me." She stood up and did a little victory dance around the kitchen on her walking sticks, then stopped to reflect what might be in store for her. "I asked for it, didn't I? Now I'll really have something to butt my head against."

That night, Timothy and I took her to her favorite Greek restaurant to celebrate. Since she'd already made plans to go out with Rupert, we invited him to join us.

Lately I'd wondered whether he and Eileen might be lovers. If so, they were sleeping together at Rupert's place, not ours.

He was quiet all evening, which wasn't like him. While we were having a last cup of coffee and I was gazing at Eileen's and Timothy's faces in the soft candlelight, the idea that I was going to be separated from these people I loved so much was like a millstone I had to pretend wasn't there. Glancing across the table, I saw the same weighted cheerfulness in Rupert's face, and knew he was feeling the same thing I was. His eyes met mine.

IN MAY, NELL FLEW north for my commencement, and also attended Timothy's when she found out his parents hadn't been able to make the trip. That evening she told me how much she liked him. "It's obvious he's good for you. What does he plan to do after—"

"Teach and do research," I said quickly, not wanting to think about the intervening years.

"Is living in your small town going to be compatible with that?"

"I don't know."

Timothy and I hadn't talked much about the future. I think we both knew there was no point until he'd finished the fellowship.

On our last day together, we made love. I kept trying to hold his hands, yet at the same time I wanted them touching me everywhere. We had learned each other so deeply.

After seeing him off on another dismal Greyhound bus, I wandered around campus hating the sunshine, the blue May sky, and, most of all, couples.

The next day as Eileen and I were packing to move out of the Benvenue house, she kept looking at me worriedly. Finally she said, "Nora, we'll write, we'll talk on the phone, we won't lose touch, you'll see."

I nodded, hoping desperately it would be that way, yet glimpsing my old familiar darkness on the horizon.

THAT SUMMER I WAS BACK at Nell's, working at the zoo and

sending applications to veterinary schools in the east, when I received word from Davis that one of the graduate students they'd accepted had dropped out. I'd been accepted in his place.

I drove up in mid-August. The contrast to Berkeley was sharp; a flat, yellow landscape surrounding a town of carefully cultivated trees, unnatural in that hot, dry climate. Yet the graduate students' complexions were so pale, I concluded they spent most of their time in the libraries.

I found a spartan, one-room apartment within walking distance of the animal husbandry buildings where I'd be spending most of my time and by the end of my first week, was putting in twelve-hour days, feeling as if I lived on an island surrounded by books and microscopes.

Timothy and Eileen were working hard, too.

Timothy's letters revealed his homesickness for the west. In one, he wrote, "The light on the Charles River seems filtered with gray compared to the light on California rivers; even the ivy here is a more somber green." He was scheduled to leave for the Persian Gulf at the end of the first semester, sometime in February.

Eileen's clerkship was so demanding that she had little time to write, so we got in the habit of calling each other two or three times a week after midnight, when the rates were low. I'd grab a snack and plump up the pillows on my bed and settle in just like I used to when we stayed up talking half the night in the Benvenue house. She was being given "no quarter" for her MS, which pleased her. "I have to double, sometimes triple check every citation." But her weekly conferences with the judge, during which "he probes my political ideology," did not make her happy. "He's like a damn surgeon, deciding where to make the first cut."

I'D HOPED TIMOTHY MIGHT come west for Christmas, and I planned to fly to Boulder if he made it that far. But his work at Harvard and the training regime for the Gulf were too intense. He left for Oman, the site of the first environmental investigation, in mid-February. Every time he called, the line was filled with so much static, we could barely hear each another. But he wrote whenever he could, describing his barracks-mate, Ken, from Oregon, as "utterly likeable" and saying the biologist in charge of the team "cracks a wicked work whip, but that's okay because we're riding the heels of the hounds of hell. Sandstorms from the *shamal* winds acted as oil-sinking agents in the Gulf after the war, and when the sludge settled on the bottom, it suffocated a lot of living things. Almost all the marsh grasses were wiped out. On the land, seedbanks were destroyed. I'm told farmers fleeing their fields ate the seeds to survive."

WHEN I WENT HOME at the end of my first year of veterinary school, Nell's worried expression told me she understood that the way I looked couldn't be blamed solely on graduate student fatigue.

Staying with her helped ease my deep loneliness. But even after I'd been home a couple of weeks, I was still exhausted and sleeping so soundly, I didn't hear the phone when it rang in the hall outside my room in the early morning hours. Nell had to shake me.

"What is it?" I asked, struggling awake.

"It's Timothy."

I sat up. "What's wrong? Where is he calling from?"

"I don't know."

I went into the hall, scared and apprehensive. Something must be wrong. Why else would he be calling at this hour?

"Timothy?"

"Heron, Ken just yelled at me it's only four o'clock in the morning in California. I'm sorry if I scared you. God, it's good to hear your voice."

"Where are you?"

"At Harvard. We got back last night."

"Is everything okay?"

"Everything's great. We're being given some time off. Ken is driving west and wants a co-driver. Are you free? I was hoping we could go camping on Santa Cruz Island."

Unable to answer, I was struck by what an extraordinary thing it is to be silenced by joy.

"Heron?"

"Yes," I said, and then louder, "Yes!" And I sat down on the floor, holding the telephone cord as if it were a lifeline. "When will you come?"

"We should be on your aunt's doorstep around the middle of June."

"It's been a year," I said dumbly.

"I know."

"Have you changed?"

"I'm balder."

I laughed.

"What about you?"

"Nell says I have sharp corners, and I'm starting to look like a book."

"Well, we'll try and soften you up."

A beat of silence. Then, "I guess I don't want to say any more until we're face-to-face, except . . . Heron, I've missed you so much."

Tears washed my cheeks.

"See you," he said.

I held onto the phone a few more minutes, then went back to my room and sat at my desk until sunrise colored the leaves of the jacaranda tree outside.

ON THE SEVENTH OF JUNE, the doorbell rang in the early evening. I knew it couldn't be Timothy, yet I ran to the door and opened it and there he stood, all six feet three inches of him, his balding head and gaunt face more beautiful to me than ever. He opened his arms, and we just held onto each other until Nell came into the entrance hall. I drew Timothy inside, and he gave Nell a quick, shy peck on the cheek.

She said, "I'm very glad you're here," and turning to leave, added, "I'll be out back if anybody needs me—which I doubt."

I led Timothy upstairs to my room. He put down his knapsack and told me he and Ken had decided to drive straight through to California and were planning to stop in Boulder on the way back. He stood gazing at my old oak desk, my shelves of books, and the jacaranda tree, then turned to me and murmured, "Heron," and we were home.

During those feasting days at Nell's, we ate and talked and walked and shopped for camping supplies. Timothy knew Santa Cruz Island from working there summers during his first two years at Berkeley, and he entertained Nell and me with its lore, making it sound like a place in another galaxy. He said he'd show me scrub jays bigger and bluer than any on the mainland, island foxes smaller than house cats, and giant island buckwheat that had been there when tiny elephant-like creatures called pygmy mammoths roamed the pine forest thousands of years ago.

A charter boat made the twenty-three-mile trip from the mainland once a day during summer. Nell drove us to the boat dock in Ventura on Monday and agreed to pick us up at the end of the week.

Timothy had predicted cool, foggy mornings and sunny after-noons, and that's what we got. After breakfast, we took long walks on the north-facing slopes where the fog-drenched chaparral was like gray-green velvet.

We swam away the sunlit afternoons, sometimes scuba-diving for hours. The long twilit evenings were for lovemaking, and there were moments when it was as if the months of separation had never been. Timothy whooped with joy when he found a small cluster of Santa Cruz Island Live-Forever in a patch of prairie grass. That night, he told me the story of the Barberry Ants. He said that twenty-five thousand years ago, a land bridge connected Asia and North America. Ants carried wild barberry seeds across that bridge, and that's why Asian wild barberry grows in the Pacific Northwest today. "Think of it, Heron," he whispered, "those nearsighted soldiers trudging thousands of miles with their backpacks of seeds."

But other times, the things he had seen in the gulf haunted him into deep silence. The expression in his eyes became bleak, and the lonely year just past and the one looming ahead enclosed us.

Most mornings I was aware of him getting up before dawn and leaving the tent. On our last day, I followed and found him sitting on the bluff staring out at the ocean, tossing a small pebble from one hand to the other. Fog dimmed the stars.

"Timothy?"

He turned.

"Can you talk about it?"

He didn't answer.

I went to sit beside him, wrapping the blanket I'd brought around both of us. "Is the reason you won't talk about it because I don't . . . because I'm not . . ."

"Heron, it's because I don't want it to be here with us."

"But it is. It's like some stranger you keep leaving me to be with."

"I know," he whispered. "I'm sorry."

"Don't be sorry. *Talk* to me."

He put his hands in the pockets of his windbreaker. He was shivering as he described some of what he'd seen: "Ever since the war, the monsoons have been weird. So many things are dying or in jeopardy. The coral reefs grow more vulnerable every year. There used to be a seacow called a dugong—said to be the origin of mermaid legends. Nobody has seen one since the war back in 1991. A town called Al Wafrah, where farmers grew fruit and vegetables—I think it must have been a lot like Salinas—is a ghost town. Oil and explosives detonated during the war caused metals to settle in the ground. They've contaminated the soil and vegetation. There are no farmers, no crops. One thing has affected another and another until you believe there can be no end to the harm that was done."

We left the island that afternoon. As the charter boat approached the mainland, Timothy's face looked drawn.

We made love in my room that night. A few hours later, I woke to see him standing by my desk, looking out the dark window.

DURING THE FALL AND winter months, he called and wrote often from Harvard, sounding more like his old self. Then it was time for the team to go overseas again. This year they would be headquartered first in Qatar and then Kuwait.

I only got one letter. It said, "I have trouble writing you here, Heron, because whenever I put pen to paper, the horror spills out. The drought is more severe this year, which is the opposite of what everyone hoped. And the rain has been so acidic, crops won't grow. People and animals are starving. But the team works hard, and we shore up each other's morale. I've made friends with a fisherman and a farmer who gave me some seeds, and I spend as much time with them as I can. I do think constantly about being with you. And one day soon, I will be."

SEEDLINGS

"One nub of growth
Nudges a sand-crumb loose
Pokes through a musty sheath
Its pale tendrilous horn."

THEODORE ROETHKE

imothy was killed in Kuwait.

His friend Ken wrote, telling me that Timothy had been walking on the beach with a fisherman when an old concealed land mine had exploded, killing both of them.

Ken's letter said, "I was the one they asked to go through his things, and I found this. I thought you should have it." He'd enclosed a small box wrapped in brown paper.

I tore up the letter and put the box in the back of a bureau drawer. Then I buried Timothy in the same emotional crypt where I kept my parents. After that, I worked. I became a work machine. Every paper I wrote, every exam I took came back with an A+.

Eileen sent a telegram asking why I wasn't answering my telephone, and I wrote her a note telling her about Timothy. Whenever my phone rang late at night after that, I knew it was Eileen and didn't answer. But finally, one night, I did pick it up.

"Damn it, Nora!"

"I can't talk about it."

"Don't *do* this to yourself."

"Look, I'm really busy, I've got two papers due tomorrow and—"

She cut me off. "I have to ask you one thing before you hang up on me." Something knotted in her voice made me listen.

"Okay. Go ahead."

"Is the reason you haven't called because once when we were arguing, I said you couldn't keep ignoring what was going on in the world, that some day it would affect you? Because . . ." She took a deep breath. "I didn't mean . . ." her voice blurred, and I could tell she was crying. "Nora, I didn't mean Timothy."

"Of course you didn't," I said, and murmuring, "I have to go now," replaced the receiver. If I hadn't, everything would have caved in on me.

Eileen didn't call again though she wrote a letter at the beginning of summer, telling me she'd finished her clerkship and had joined a public service law firm in there Washington.

I wrote a brief congratulatory note.

I graduated from veterinary school with high honors and went to live at Nell's while I looked for a job. We didn't talk about Timothy or Eileen, but one evening as I was going upstairs to bed, Nell said, "Wait a minute, Nora." She went to the kitchen cupboard and reaching far in the back, took out two spiral notebooks. She handed them to me saying, "I don't know whether these will help. That's for you to decide."

Upstairs in my room, I opened the first one and began to read. The notebooks were journals Nell had kept after my parents died. The entries—cryptic, jagged, anguished—chronicled *her* grief. I was mesmerized. I'd always known Nell and my father had been close and that they had shared a deep love of nature. When my love of animals surfaced, Nell told me, "It's in your genes, Nora." After my father married, Nell and my mother became close as well. But I hadn't realized until now how completely Nell's life had been interwoven with my parents'. I stayed up most of the night reading and rereading her journal—pulled closer to my aunt, and, strangely, to my parents.

I thanked her the next day.

She said, "I respect privacy, Nora. You know that. But don't forsake the living. Eileen may need you."

I nodded, but I couldn't make the call. Eileen and I had shared too much that was over.

During the summer, working with the placement bureau at Davis, I went on several job interviews, but none of the clinics felt right. Then in mid-September, I received a letter from Dr. Jake Overby, owner of a rural animal practice in the town of Combsea near the California-Oregon border. He was a Davis alumnus, too, and was looking for an associate. We set up an interview. He told me Combsea, population around twenty-five hundred, had been named for the Combsea River, which ran from the mountains to ocean. The town lay midway between the rich, agricultural Clear Creek Valley and the Siskiyou Mountain timberlands. The old state highway, California 96, winding through the Klamath National Forest would take me to a three-mile cut-off leading to Combsea.

Nell had given me a Jeep as a graduation present, and this trip would be its baptism. I drove as far as Yreka the first day, spent the night, rose at dawn, and entered the forest just as the sun was lighting the tops of the trees. Except for an occasional logging truck whooshing past, the old highway was deserted and incredibly beautiful. Red and brown and yellow leaves drifting off of maples swirled on windgusts across the road; gnarled oaks and pines bowed to the land. Where the trees backed away from the roadside, mosses and ferns decorated the shale rock—pewter-colored in sunlight, amethyst in the shade. Wild grasses that Timothy would have known the names of. . . .

I gripped the steering wheel and silenced that.

The cut-off from the highway wound through dense forest to a community nestled between mountains on one side and sloping meadowland on the other. Rural mailboxes were clustered together every mile or so. On the outskirts of the town, an old steepled church guarded an overgrown cemetery. Driving slowly down the main street, I saw a red brick bank building with an old-fashioned balcony and a tower clock that was fifteen minutes slow.

Following Dr. Overby's directions, I came to the clinic—a one-story building two blocks south of Main. Turning into a graveled parking lot shaded by a large madrone tree, I parked the Jeep next to a pick-up with "Combsea Animal Clinic" painted on the door.

A tall man with a weather-beaten face came to the outer reception room and introduced himself as Jake Overby. Murmuring gruffly, "You're right on time," he led me down the hallway to his office. His dark brown hair was touched with gray, and his thick eyebrows accentuated thoughtful eyes.

In the course of the next couple of hours, I could tell from the questions he asked, and the intent way he listened to my answers, how deeply he cared about his clinic. Near the end of the afternoon he paused to study the yellow tablet he'd been taking notes on, and I concluded the interview must be nearly over. But standing up with a tautness that caught my attention, he moved to the window, stood staring out at his pick-up for a minute, then turned to face me. "Maybe I should have told you this before you drove up here. Winifred, my office manager, said I should." He flexed his shoulders then went on, "Winifred has been after me to get an associate for almost two years. But I decided to wait and see how a certain situation settled out. You'd better hear about it if you're interested in working here. Are you?"

None of the other towns I'd visited had evoked the feelings Combsea did. Living in these mountains would be different from anything I'd ever known. I wanted that. I also sensed I'd probably like working with this quiet, somber man. So I answered, "Yes."

He asked me, then, how much I knew about verdicides.

I'd learned about them in biology classes and knew they contained fast-acting, synthetic plant growth hormones. The hormones made plants devour light until their entire bud-growth-death cycle was condensed into minutes instead of months. Verdicides had been refined over the past decade until companies and corporations could order them created to kill whatever plants or weeds they wanted to get rid of. "Sort of like plant genocide," my professor had said.

Speaking without any expression in his voice, Jake explained, "A verdicide called Luminex is sprayed on this valley every spring to kill the manzanita and mountain laurel that steal soil nutrients from commercial timber. It's also used on weeds that damage grazing land and scrub brush that soak up rainwater needed by local farmers."

"But what does all this have to do with being a veterinarian?"

He straightened a stack of folders on his desk that didn't need straightening before he said, "Luminex causes physical defects in developing embryos." He paused, then went on quickly, "A year ago, people in the valley who wanted the spraying stopped raised about four thousand dollars to get a referendum on the ballot to ban the spraying. But they were up against owners of lumber companies, ranchers leasing huge parcels of government-owned rangeland, and utility companies."

"Utility companies?"

"Luminex is sprayed on plants that clog access to power poles and telephone lines. Well, when the referendum movement looked as if it might generate support, those businesses formed a coalition, mailed out pamphlets, took out newspaper ads, and bought TV time sending a clear message about what would happen here if they withdrew their economic support."

Telling me these things, his whole demeanor was different from when he was discussing the clinic. He'd become detached.

He said, "I imagine you know who won."

I nodded. "The big guys."

"I'm aware from your resume you grew up in Los Angeles and attended . . . UC Berkeley."

I didn't miss the pause.

"Since you've never lived in a small town, you may not know how things like this settle out. People here are basically stoic. After the referendum movement was defeated, most simply went along with that. So you need to understand, anyone who works with the animal population here has to be able to accept whatever she or he encounters."

"Including animals born deformed," I said.

He nodded.

I crossed and uncrossed my legs. "I've never had to deal with that."

"And you may not have to here. It doesn't happen often. But I can't have someone in my practice who turns around and leaves because he or she can't handle it. Or who decides to try and change things."

Since I didn't envision myself trying to change a thing, I was startled at how much I resented being told not to. I also couldn't believe Jake's remoteness. Those sad lines in his face hadn't come from being indifferent.

Then he told me, "I almost didn't respond to your resume."

"Why?"

He didn't answer right away.

"Because I'm a woman?"

He looked surprised. "No."

Then I remembered his hesitation when he'd mentioned Berkeley. The reputation of that campus had probably been very much alive while he was at Davis. "Were you afraid I might be a rabble rouser?" I smiled.

"Something like that."

"Well, I'm not. I intend to practice good veterinary medicine. That's as far as my life plan goes."

The dark eyes still seemed to weigh me as he absentmindedly rubbed the lines on his forehead. "Would you be willing to sign an agreement with a separation clause?"

This was a new development. "I don't know," I answered.

"Either of us could activate it during the first year. I think it would be a good idea."

"Does that mean you're offering me the position?"

"I believe we should try each other out."

I glanced past him out the window at the quiet street, the forest, and snow-tipped mountains in the distance.

"Do you need some time?" he asked.

I took a deep breath. "No. I'm willing to try it out."

He smiled then, a boyish grin that changed his face so much, it startled me. "When can you start?"

Today was Monday. I'd have to find a place to live in Combsea, go back to Nell's, pack, and so on. I had no idea how long all that would take, but I said optimistically, "A week from today."

"Good. Now come and meet Winifred. She runs the place."

As we walked down the hallway toward the front of the clinic, Jake told me Winifred had been a nurse in Santa Rosa for over twenty years. After reaching retirement age, she'd moved to Combsea. Finding herself, as she put it, "rusting from disuse," she'd started looking around for something to do. One day she brought her nasty-tempered tomcat in to have an abscess lanced. Observing the disarray in the waiting room with a professional eye, she'd told Jake it was obvious he needed help. That was fifteen years ago, and, "She's been running my life ever since," he finished, opening the door to her office.

Jake's description had led me to expect someone stern and forbidding. Winifred was a fragile-looking woman with wispy white hair and bright blue eyes. As she stood to greet us, I judged she couldn't be over five-foot-two. She gripped my hand in response to Jake's introduction, saying, "Welcome," and I felt her strength. As her eyes darted from me to him, I sensed she was the clinic's protector and maybe Jake's, too.

JAKE AND I DISCUSSED the terms of our contract over lunch and agreed on a one-year separation clause stipulating that either of us could dissolve the association by giving the other sixty days' notice. Jake said he'd have his attorney draw up the agreement.

It was almost three o'clock when we finished, and I used the remaining daylight hours to explore Combsea. Downtown was the equivalent of ten city blocks long. Besides the old brick bank building, there were a couple of small markets, a bakery, a drugstore, a post office, a hardware store, the feed and tack store across from the clinic, two bars (one at each end of town), a coffee shop, an Italian restaurant, a curio gift shop, two churches, and a motel. It looked like a town that hadn't changed since the forties.

I took a room at the motel and told the proprietor I was looking for a house to rent. She suggested I read the bulletin boards in the post office and markets, and if I didn't find anything, that I try a real estate office in the county seat of Clarksville twelve miles away.

But the next morning I did find an ad on the post office bulletin board for a house on the outskirts of town. I called the owner, told him I was going to be working at the animal clinic, and made an appointment. The house turned out to be a rustic cabin—basically one huge, pine-walled room with a small kitchen, bath, and sleeping alcove —sitting in the middle of its own forested acre. It was about three miles from Combsea on the opposite side of town from the clinic, and though it was only half a mile off the highway, the pine and fir trees surrounding it made it seem much farther.

The owner, Henry Mahler, told me I'd be glad the highway was so close if we had a snowy winter because state work crews kept the highway clear. He was short and wiry, an 87-year-old retired mail-route driver who'd had to move into town when his bones stiffened up from arthritis.

His faded eyes seemed nonjudgmental as he said, "So you're going to be Jake Overby's helper?"

"His associate, yes."

"Jake's a good vet."

"I got that impression."

"I never met a lady vet."

"Until now."

He chuckled, then told me proudly he'd built the cabin himself, and that it was constructed of twelve-inch, hand-hewn logs, the corners were fully dovetailed, the roof didn't leak, and the wind stayed outside where it belonged.

I think even if the roof had had holes in it, I would have rented that cabin. I signed a year's lease, and after Henry left, went outside and stood on the front porch. Before I knew it, Timothy's voice was inside my mind, naming the trees in the pine grove: Douglas fir, digger pine. . . . Seeing the way their branches touched, I turned away and walked back to my Jeep.

At the motel, I made calls to have the electricity and gas connected and a telephone installed. The soonest any of the utility people could promise was Thursday, and they said more likely it would be Friday.

Leaving Combsea around noon, I drove steadily south, stopping only for gas. It was almost midnight when I reached Santa Monica. Entering Nell's house, I didn't even try to be quiet; I wanted her to wake up so I could tell her my news.

She came downstairs in her blue kimono, her short, gray hair tousled from sleep. As we sat at the kitchen table where we'd thrashed out so many problems, I was aware how much I owed this woman. She listened quietly as I described the town, Jake, Winifred, the clinic, and the house I'd rented in the woods. But it disturbed me that I didn't mention Luminex—even though Jake had said that was a settled issue.

Nell leaned across the table, took my face between her hands, gave me a little shake, and murmured, "Good for you, Nora. It sounds like you found exactly what you wanted."

I slept until almost noon, and Nell stayed in her studio when I got up. Purposefully, I think, she kept on working late into the afternoon, letting me have the house to myself to sort through my past and future.

Deciding what to take or leave behind, I started with the easy things. I'd felt a crisp coldness in the Combsea air, chillier than anything I'd experienced in Berkeley, so I packed my warmest clothes. Next I sorted through my books, putting ones I wanted to take with me in boxes. Then I stood staring at the desk where I'd spent so many hours studying, talking on the phone to Eileen, writing letters to Timothy, and I did what I'd been putting off ever since I'd gotten up that morning. I went to my bureau, opened the middle drawer, reached far into the back and took out Nell's journals, Timothy's letters, and the box Ken had sent. Then I went downstairs and got the photo album of my parents out of the dining room buffet. I put them all inside the bottom drawer of my desk, and shut the drawer sharply. They were ballast. I needed them with me.

After making arrangements to have the desk and other things I couldn't pack shipped, I carried boxes downstairs and loaded them into my Jeep. Knowing I was too excited to sleep, I decided to start out that night.

Nell gave me a hamper containing sandwiches and a thermos of coffee for the journey. We'd said other goodbyes—when I'd gone away to Berkeley and then Davis. But this one was different, and we both knew it.

Fighting tears, I said, "I'll miss you."

She put her arms around me and held me tightly for a moment. "The holiday season isn't far away," she said quickly. "We'll see each other then."

I nodded. Then I told her I'd taken the photograph album.

She smiled. "Good."

She walked with me to the door and stood beneath the porch lamp watching as I drove away.

WHEN I REACHED COMBSEA, I drove straight to the cabin, unrolled my sleeping bag on the floor, crawled into it, and slept until the telephone man woke me by knocking. He seemed shy and went about his work with an earnest expression, careful not to ask any questions beyond the information he needed for the phone company. His eyebrows went up a little when I told him I was a veterinarian.

After he left, I stood staring at my new telephone, then glanced at the clock on the wall. It wasn't yet six in the east, and I'd memorized the name of the law firm. But I needed more time; I didn't even know myself yet in this place.

I stepped out onto my front porch. A soft wind rocked the branches of the pine trees. A pair of goldfinches called to each other. Soon I gave myself over to the sunlight slanting onto my face and the pine smell all around me. When the sun began to disappear behind the treetops and the air grew chilly and the shadows long, I went into my house. My house.

ONE EVENING IN BERKELEY, after listening to me describe the kind of town I hoped to practice in, Eileen had said no such place existed. Well, perhaps I'd proven her wrong. It seemed over the next weeks that I'd left a whole culture behind—the noise, the pace, the mottled air, the panic.

Having walked on concrete most of my life, the crunch and smell of pine needles beneath my feet was intoxicating. Gradually, my ears overcame the conditioning of twenty-five years' exposure to city noise, and I began to distinguish between a rodent rustle and insect skitter. As the autumn days grew shorter, added to the things I loved was the texture of the Combsea nights—a flawless black unbroken by street-lights or neon.

Late fall approaching winter is usually a quiet time for animals, and even the clinic seemed serene as I familiarized myself with the clients and routine. Winifred was helpful, though I sometimes felt she was uneasy toward me, and I had no idea why. However, Jake and I were as good a match as I'd hoped, sharing an affinity for silence and intense concentration. He was gentler than any veterinarian I'd worked with during my internship, but at the same time deft and intuitive, as though his fingers had invisible antennae. We talked very little while we worked, and then only about the animals we were treating. But sometimes, sharing a cup of coffee in the narrow room between our offices that housed supply cupboards, filing cabinets, and a percolator, we'd chat.

Jake told me funny stories about the basset hound named Magruder he lived with, confirming my intuition he was a bachelor (or, perhaps, a widower?). I related some of my experiences with zoo animals, pleased whenever I made him laugh because it softened his face so much and I had the feeling he didn't laugh often. Neither of us revealed much about our personal lives. I didn't talk about Eileen or Timothy, and Jake didn't tell me about anybody either.

When he started taking me along with him to visit ranches and farms, I was a little apprehensive. During my internship, I'd run into a few ranchers around Davis who felt uneasy with a woman veterinarian. Surprisingly, most were young men. The grizzled ones didn't give a damn about gender as long as their animals were treated right. I wondered if I would encounter similar resistance among any of Jake's clients.

There was some. I'd catch it in the way certain ranchers' eyes veered away from meeting mine, or their hesitation before leading me into a barn or a birthing pasture. But they liked Jake so much they were willing to try and accept me. So as soon as I'd proved what I could do inside and outside the clinic, Jake said he and Winifred would spend a couple of evenings deciding which clients to turn over to me.

It took longer than a couple of evenings, almost a week, and it seemed to me that there was tension between them while they were doing it. But finally Jake handed me the list one morning. Studying Winifred's neatly typed sheet, I was pleased to see Paul Milo's name. He'd bought his small dairy ranch a couple of years ago, and when Jake introduced us, he'd held out his hand, saying "Meet another newcomer." He was about my height, large-boned and solid-looking, and I liked his face. If Nell were sketching him, I think she would have concentrated on the nose and cheekbones. Both were strong.

Continuing down the list, I noticed Marilyn O'Hare's brood mare ranch penciled in at the bottom, and I remarked how eager I was to be taking on my first big client.

Winifred asked smoothly if she could see the list for a second and after I handed it to her, she scanned it, gave it back, then shot Jake a glance I would have missed if I'd blinked. Jake ignored it. His brow furrowing, he said, "Actually, Marilyn might not have a lot of work for you." Then he explained that two years ago, Luminex drifting across the valley on windgusts had settled on the O'Hare ranch. The following spring, several of Marilyn's mares had birthed stillborn, deformed foals. She placed her ranch on a breeding moratorium and devoted her time to the movement to get the Luminex referendum on the ballot. When that failed, she'd continued the moratorium despite the economic hardship it imposed. Rumor around the valley now was that she was selling off her brood mares one by one and ultimately might have to sell the ranch.

This was the first time Jake had mentioned Luminex since the day of my interview, and it was obvious from the way he wouldn't meet my eyes that it made him uncomfortable. He changed the subject to tell me he would bring my primary care clients up to half the clinic's total once I got through my first spring in Combsea. Yet that statement had a dark underside, too. Winifred had given me the spraying schedule. Spring, the mating and birthing season, was also when the spraying occurred.

At home that night, sitting at my desk gazing out the window at the Combsea dark, loneliness crept into the cabin. I glanced at the phone and then the clock. It was our old calling time. But I couldn't call her after midnight now. Too many months had passed.

Arguing with myself, I leaned down to the bottom drawer of the desk, and took out the photo album of my parents. Turning through it slowly, I stared at their faces. They stared back, unable to see me, almost as if I were the ghost. Closing the album, putting it back, my fingers brushed the coarse brown wrapping paper on the package Ken had sent. I drew back, shut the drawer, and hurried into the sleeping alcove.

DURING THE NEXT FEW WEEKS, my work intensified mentally and physically as I got acquainted with my clients. Some were reserved, withholding judgment, I felt, until I'd proven myself. Others were immediately outgoing and friendly. Like Paul Milo.

The day I went to his ranch to help him dehorn some calves, he told me he'd moved to Combsea from the Imperial Valley after losing his land there to developers. He said, "I've fought a lot of battles, but they were all paltry compared to those guys. I lost."

Acutely aware of the strength emanating from this man, I said, "Still, I bet they knew they were in a fight."

He grinned. "Yeah." Then he said, "Not to brag, but I'm a better-than-average dancer. Maybe you'd like to go to a shindig in Clarksville some evening?"

I smiled. "Maybe."

"Okay. I'll call you."

I nodded. Driving back to the clinic, I wondered if he really would.

As soon as I'd mastered my caseload, Winifred made up a new schedule. If there were no emergencies, Jake would come in early in the morning, stock up on supplies, and do his out-of-office calls before noon while I treated animals at the clinic; then I did my out-of-office calls in the afternoons while he stayed in. Most days, we brushed by each other in the hall at lunchtime and at the end of the day with a "How's it going?" On Friday afternoons we took time to discuss any cases we needed to confer on. I was puzzled by the let-down feeling I had after those Friday sessions until I realized where it was coming from. Now that I was pretty much on my own with my clients, I missed Jake's company.

Despite the gnawing loneliness, work made the days pass so swiftly I could scarcely believe it when I realized Thanksgiving was approaching. Nell had said she'd try to come north for the long weekend, but she was illustrating a book by a new author, and as it turned out, she wasn't able to get away.

Monday of Thanksgiving week, Winifred surprised me by stopping by the door of my office and saying, "Nora, since your aunt can't come to Combsea, I don't think Jake would mind if you took a few days off to go home."

On the surface, at least, it was the friendliest thing she'd said since I'd been working there. But my mind snagged on the word "home." Nell's house wasn't home any more; Combsea was. Also Nell would be busy, and the long drive back and forth over snowy roads didn't appeal to me nearly as much as my cabin. So I told Winifred I'd be staying in Combsea, and even considered inviting her to my house for Thanksgiving dinner with the thought of easing some of the mysterious tension between us. But, spoiled by Nell into never having to cook anything complicated, I decided against it. That and the fact that I anticipated being called out on at least a couple of emergencies also discouraged me from inviting Paul Milo or Jake. That's what I told myself.

I did wonder if Jake had been invited somewhere for dinner. By then I knew he lived in a big white clapboard house on the edge of town that had belonged to his parents and I speculated whether his life was really as solitary as it seemed.

To my surprise, the holiday passed without my phone ringing once. For Thanksgiving dinner, I ate smoked turkey and pumpkin tarts Nell had sent me via Federal Express. Plus sourdough bread from the Combsea bakery. Drowsy by early evening, I went to bed before eight. I was wide awake on Friday at dawn and decided I might as well go to the clinic and do some catch-up work on my files.

Winifred was in her office when I got there. She looked as unsettled to see me as I was to see her.

"What is this," I said, "a workaholic's vacation?"

She gave a little shrug.

I asked, "Did the animals take a holiday, too? I didn't get any emergency calls."

Giving me a look I couldn't fathom, she said, "There were a few. Jake took them."

"*Why?*" I demanded. "I was available."

"Well," she said, "he wanted to. It's still his clinic, you know."

"Seems like it's yours to me," I almost snapped, but walked away instead, surprised at just how hard it was for me to do that.

AS CHRISTMAS DREW NEAR, Nell called to tell me she doubted her problems with the new book would be resolved before Christmas day, but she promised she'd come for New Year's. The memories of all the times we'd strung chili-pepper lights on the cactus in her living room and of the rich holiday cooking smells that filled her house made me realize again just how much of a stranger I still was in this town. When I walked down Main Street, a lot of people I'd seen dozens of times looked at me without a blink of recognition.

On the other hand, Henry Mahler would always stop and chat and ask how his cabin was holding up, and Marty, who owned the feed and tack store across from the clinic, was friendly. So was Zelda in the bakery. She was from Finland—a war bride who'd come to Combsea in the forties. Her ancient cocker spaniel was prone to the problems a lot of spaniels have—ear mites and an allergic reaction to fleas—and Jake had, apparently, been keeping the animal healthy for years. So every time I went in to buy a cinnamon roll for breakfast, she'd send a piece of strudel along for him. I only caught glimpses of her husband, Ray, because he came in before dawn to do the baking and left when the bakery opened, but I'd sampled so much of what he made, I felt I knew him. And on days I really got desperate for somebody to talk to, I could buy some honey from Mavis Wilson, a gossipy beekeeper who lived on the edge of town. She was always interested in knowing whose animal had been treated for what, which often led to her discussing their owners with a kind of earnest dedication, as if she felt someone ought to keep track of the people in this town and she had volunteered. I came close, once, to asking her about Jake's personal life, and rationalizing later, blamed my holiday homesickness.

When I told Winifred I had no plans for the Christmas holiday, I added that I expected to be given some emergency calls. She just nodded coolly and said, "Fine by me."

On Christmas morning, I got a surprise when Winifred did indeed call me into the office. I had to set a compound leg fracture a wolf suffered in an encounter with a logging truck.

Wolves are still rare in Northern California. Years ago the mountains had been home to the Cascades gray wolf, but after being heavily hunted the animals had fled north to Canada. Now a few were drifting south to feed on the sprawling deer population.

Fortunately, the driver of the logging truck—a big, shy, rosy-cheeked kid—was fascinated enough by what he had hit to bring the wolf in. His expression was full of remorse as he carried the unconscious animal into the examining room. He held her while I set her leg. He looked about seventeen. He told me his name was Will Jenkins.

When the wolf began to stir, I administered a tranquilizer to keep her quiet until I could get a holding pen ready. After we'd put her in it, Will and I shared a cup of coffee. He gave me his phone number and promised he'd come back as soon as her leg had healed. "I'll drive her back up into the mountains and set her free," he said.

I'd worked on a couple of wolves during my summers at the zoo and found them fascinating, though I'd been told by the zoo's expert that wolves in captivity were completely different from those in the wild. For one thing, wolves were animals used to traveling a hundred miles a day instead of pacing around enclosures. He'd explained how their minds carried search images, sort of like the smart bombs used in the Gulf War; the equivalent of computerized coordinate grids flashed in their brains as they wove through the woods tracking their prey. He'd also talked about how invincible they were. Hunting in the wild, a lot of them suffered skull fractures, broken ribs, joint injuries —yet they survived.

In the days that followed, I went to see the wolf whenever I had a spare moment. Gazing into her eyes, so like humans' in their shape and depth, gave me the eerie feeling that I wasn't the one doing the looking.

NELL ARRIVED THREE DAYS after Christmas.

She brought me a late present, a lovely dress she'd found in a boutique in Santa Monica. It was cream-colored cotton with a full skirt and delicate lace insets in the sleeves. But I had no idea where I'd ever wear it in Combsea or even Santa Monica. When I wore dresses, which wasn't often, I chose simple ones in subdued colors. Nell had chided me for that in the past and observing the bewildered look on my face now, said, "I know, it's not how you see yourself. But I also know how lovely you would look in this dress, and I wanted you to have it. Maybe because you work so hard. At least once a decade, you should go dancing."

I thought of Paul Milo and said, "That's an interesting idea."

The next morning I took her to the clinic to meet Winifred and Jake. Jake surprised me by complimenting her on a book about otters she'd illustrated, saying it had always been a favorite.

After Jake left on rounds, I took Nell to see the wolf. She, too, was intrigued, and after that spent time with the animal almost every morning, quietly sketching. Later, while I went on working, she'd go back to the house and take long afternoon walks in my woods. Evenings, we'd sit in front of my pot-bellied stove in our pajamas and robes, reminiscing and catching up on each other's lives.

She told me she was going to be spending part of the new year in England illustrating a book of poems by a young British woman, adding, "I've always wanted to see where Beatrix Potter lived."

Our easy conversations plus the bereft feeling I had, realizing she'd soon be on the other side of the world, made me realize how hungry I was to be with someone I cared about who cared about me.

One evening Nell asked how I was getting along with Jake, and I said, "Fine. He's a good vet, great to work with."

"And outside of work?"

I picked up the poker to prod the coals inside the stove. "I don't see him outside work."

She remarked then how he seemed locked inside himself and mused, "I wonder what he was like before."

"Before what?"

"Before he changed."

I puzzled over that for a couple of moments, then asked what she meant.

"Well, some people's lives maintain a steady course. But when certain others experience good fortune or bad, the direction of their lives alters forever; they change, and looking back, there's always a sense of 'before' and 'after.' "

"Like when people you care about die."

Our eyes met and she nodded.

"And you think something like that happened to Jake?"

"I think so, yes. But sometimes I speculate too much." She smiled. "It probably comes from working with authors."

We were silent for a while. Then she asked about Eileen, and, again, I had to admit I hadn't been in touch.

"Not even a Christmas card?"

"No."

"Why not?"

My shrug was defensive.

Getting up swiftly and moving so she faced me, Nell said sternly, "Talk about being locked inside one's self. You've done some healing in this place, Nora. Enough so that you should be able to tell Eileen about your life here."

It was the closest thing to an order she'd ever given me. I waited for my anger to come, but it didn't. I murmured, "I'll call her."

"When?"

"This week."

"Good. Do it."

The day Nell left, I hung the dress she'd given me in the back of my closet. Wandering glumly around the empty cabin, I found two of her wolf sketches on my bureau with a note: "One of these is for you; the other is Eileen's."

It took several evenings sitting at my desk, staring out at the night, searching for the right words before I wrote, "I miss you" across the top of the page, then told her about Combsea, Jake, the clinic, etc. I put Nell's sketch and my letter inside a box containing pine cones, potpourri from mountain wildflowers, and a honeycomb from Mavis's bee farm.

Eileen called the day she got the package. The months of silence and the thousands of miles that separated us melted away as her words and mine bounced off each other. Not hearing the enthusiasm I'd expected as she described her work, I wondered if she was overdoing, so I had to ask, "Are you all right?"

"I have all my fingers and toes if that's what you mean," she replied testily. "But they treat me as if I were made of cotton candy. It's the MS that worries them. I've started asking them to call me 'Mallory' in case they're translating 'Eileen' as 'I-lean.' I really believe they're afraid to assign me a case that might involve a lengthy trial. The most important job I've had so far was defending a transient whose rights were breached when he was picked up on a vagrancy charge. What a client! This character was looking forward to being in jail for a while so he could get regular meals."

"Maybe that's just the way it has to be in the beginning," I murmured.

"Well, what about you? Are you restricted to cats and parakeets?"

"No, but—"

"But what?"

Her question touched a nerve. Ever since Thanksgiving I'd had the feeling something wasn't right. I just didn't know what.

"Nothing," I said. Then, "Listen, why don't you take a trip here? The whole time I've known you, you've never taken a vacation."

She chuckled. "Neither have you."

"Will you think about it?"

"Yes."

But I knew better than to ask when she might come.

NEAR THE MIDDLE OF FEBRUARY, I decided to release the wolf. I wasn't positive her fracture had completely healed, but she was losing weight rapidly, and if I kept her in captivity much longer, she might die.

I called Will Jenkins who said he'd borrow his father's pick-up, come to the clinic at sunup, drive the wolf up into the mountains, and set her free. I asked if he'd mind if I came along, and he said, "Heck no."

That evening, I mixed a tranquilizer in her food so I could get close enough to inject her with an anesthetic. After it took effect, I cut the cast off and put her in a transportable kennel.

Will arrived at dawn as he'd promised. Sitting beside him as he drove his truck up narrow back logging roads I hadn't even known existed, I saw green tips of mountain crocus starting to show through snow patches in the high meadows. I realized I'd soon be experiencing my first spring in Combsea, and thoughts about Luminex began to nibble the edges of my mind.

I glanced at Will. He was wearing a baseball cap with the bill turned backward. He hadn't shaved that morning; his beard stubble was a much lighter brown than his hair, and soft-looking, like Timothy's. Pushing away thoughts of Timothy, I concentrated on Will. Doubting I'd have another chance to talk to him after this journey, and because I was curious, I asked him what he thought about Luminex and the spraying.

Frowning, he hesitated. "Well, my dad says it's good for logging."
"Why?"
"Since they've been using it, we get a bigger yield of cuttable trees."
"I see."

We rode in silence for a while. The way Will kept glancing at the cassette player beneath the dashboard made me suspect that if I hadn't been there, he would have had it on at a high decibel level. Tapes were piled in a wooden box on the floor. Some I recognized from Rupert's collection: Guns 'n' Roses, U2, Cowboy Junkies. I probably would have told him to go ahead and put a tape in except it would have been hard on the wolf.

Occasionally I turned around to look at her through the rear window.
"How's she doing?" Will asked.
"Okay."
"Couple more miles and we'll set her free."

I nodded.

And then, because he seemed to care so much about animals and I didn't know whether he was aware Luminex could hurt them, I explained it could deform fetuses and asked what he thought about that.

He didn't respond until he'd pulled over to the side of the road. Then he said, "I guess that's just the way it has to be. You know, if it comes down to loggers being able to work or animals losing some of their young, well, we have to work. We have families, too."

Obviously anxious to change the subject, he gestured beyond the roadside. "This seems like a good place. What do you think?"

I looked out. I'd never been so high up on the mountain. There was quite a bit of snow on the ground, and the forest around us was beautiful, the pines a shade of green I'd never seen. Mountain laurel, which wasn't allowed to grow on the lower slopes, clustered around them.

"It's fine."

We got out of the truck then, and I helped Will pull the kennel out of the back and carry it to a clearing near the side of the road. As he was undoing the wires holding the hasp, I asked, "Do they spray up here?"

"Nope, 'cause we don't log up this high," he said brusquely. Then he knelt in front of the kennel. "You ready?"

"Well, *she* is."

He undid the hasp on the kennel door, let it fall open, and backed quickly away.

For one frozen moment, the wolf didn't move. The next, she was out and running with hardly a limp, disappearing silently through the trees. I began to picture her journey back to her companions. Will did, too; I could see it in his face.

Riding back down the mountain, we were silent most of the way. I reflected on his answers about the spraying. They had been so easy. But what did he really know? And I, a newcomer, probably knew even less.

E M E R G E N C E

"It

moratorium means well what

you think it means you

Dense? Stop it means stop.

We move and we march sing songs

move march sing songs move march move

It/stop means stop."

JUNE JORDAN

n a cold crisp afternoon at the end of February, I received my first call from the O'Hare ranch. Marilyn O'Hare's hired hand, Mel, called to tell me one of their mares had suffered several deep puncture wounds in an encounter with a porcupine. I told him I'd be there in an hour and went to inform Winifred where I was going. Glancing quickly at her schedule, she said Jake could probably take the call.

It wasn't the first time she'd shuffled things around so I'd take one of Jake's calls or vice versa. And whenever I asked why she did it, she'd reply it was due to one of us being closer to a given ranch, or Jake's experience with a particular animal. But each time it happened, I had that uneasy feeling of something being wrong. This time I knew for a fact Jake wasn't anywhere near the O'Hare ranch, and I said so, adding firmly, "The O'Hare ranch is my client, and I'm going out there."

She started to respond, then stopped. Her eyes were like blue ice chips. But she turned back to her computer without another word.

Driving up Gasquet Mountain Road half an hour later, I noticed that the green of the trees in the near distance wasn't anything like the green of the trees on the mountain where Will Jenkins and I had released the wolf. And near the roadside, the vegetation was dun-colored, sparse, and stunted-looking. Abruptly I realized I was in a spraying area.

After I'd gone about seven more miles, I came to the split-rail fence bordering the ranch. Where it ended, a carved wooden sign next to a double gate announced, O'Hare Brood Mares. I drove through the gate, passed a weathered ranchhouse, then saw a barn with sides the color of fog mist on a river. I parked in a nearby clearing and, as I walked toward the barn, called, "Anybody here?"

A middle-aged woman in overalls came out to greet me. When I'd visited the ranch a month earlier with Jake, I'd met Mel, but Marilyn had been away. She was about the same height I was. Her auburn hair was coiled in thick braids, and she had almost as many freckles as I did. Gripping my hand warmly as I introduced myself, she said, "Mel told me how much he liked you. I knew I'd trust Jake's choice of an associate. I'm also glad he chose a woman."

She led me into the barn, and I worked for two hours pulling porcupine quills from the right foreleg of a feisty roan filly. After I'd finished, Marilyn took me on a tour of her ranch, telling me Mel had been the only employee she'd kept on after her breeding moratorium. She tolerated his love of bourbon because he took such excellent care of her stock. She had Tennessee Walkers and Morgans, and they were beautiful animals, their coats glossy, eyes bright, their movements quick and spirited.

Most northern California horse breeders breed their stock in early spring and the mares deliver their foals the following spring. Normally, at least half of the O'Hare brood stock would have been heavy with foal by now. But all were barren.

A lot of things had been wearing away at my firm resolve to encapsulate Luminex as something I didn't have to deal with. After seeing the mares, I knew I couldn't do that any more.

"How long can you go on like this?" I asked, realizing immediately how intrusive the question must seem.

"Have you ever helped birth a deformed foal, Nora?"

I shook my head.

"I hope you never have to. It's a singular kind of agony. I'll do anything to avoid having to go through that again."

"But Jake said if you keep on with your moratorium, you might lose your ranch."

"Some days, I'm even willing to risk that."

"But that's not fair!"

"No," she agreed, "it isn't. But fairness seems to have very little to do with it. And I'm not down for the count yet."

"What more can you do?"

"I'm still trying to figure that out."

She walked with me to the Jeep, and I told her I'd be back to check on the roan in about a week. In my rearview mirror, I saw her raise one hand to shield her eyes from the cold February sunlight as she watched me drive away. She stood tall and straight. Despite the situation she was in the middle of, she seemed indomitable.

Marilyn stayed in my mind partly because her barren horses haunted me, but also I wanted to get to know her better. Her strength and forthrightness reminded me of Nell, who was in England now. She sent great postcards, which I would have enjoyed more if they hadn't reminded me of how far away she was.

The day I went back to check the filly, Marilyn and I sat talking for a while in her kitchen. She told me about growing up in Combsea and taking over the ranch after her father died. "We had plenty of problems twenty years ago," she said, "but they were solvable. You could work on them. By yourself, if you had to. You need consensus to tackle some things that happen now, and that's damn hard to come by, especially when people are afraid."

Driving home, reflecting on what she'd said, I thought about Jake's unease whenever the subject of Luminex came up, and I wondered if part of that was due to fear. And if so, what, exactly, was he afraid of . . . something inside himself, or in that valley, or both?

A COUPLE OF EVENINGS LATER, Paul Milo called. It was the first time we'd talked on the phone, which may be why I was so conscious of the deep, resonant texture of his voice. "I haven't forgotten about us going dancing, Nora. But the cows have conspired to keep me on the ranch."

"I know how that goes."

"So, do you like mushrooms?"

"Well, yes," I said, wondering what he was getting at.

"I have a great patch of chanterelles on a piece of my land. Want to go mushroom gathering?"

"I'm not a cook," I said.

"Hell, I am. And the god's truth is, I'm hungering for company more than I am mushrooms."

How could I resist? "I have Saturday morning off."

"Want me to pick you up?"

"No, I'll drive out. What time?"

"Seven? I'll have the milking done then. We'll go get some mushrooms, and I'll make you a great omelette."

"Deal."

The chanterelles were growing on a far corner of his ranch in the softening wood of fallen tree trunks. We gathered them slowly, enjoying the peace and quiet of the early morning, drifting in and out of easy conversation as we shared our impressions of Combsea.

Paul said, "Jake's a good guy. My first year here he let me run late on some of my bills."

I nodded.

"But Winifred—I wouldn't want to tangle with *her* in a dark alley."

I laughed.

He sat back on the ground, the pan of mushrooms on his lap.

"What do you do for company, Nora?"

"Same thing you do, I expect." I kept on picking mushrooms and putting them into a small bowl.

"Meaning?"

"My work is my company."

"And that's enough?"

I nodded.

"Not for me."

I glanced up and for a second, our eyes held. Then I looked away, and he said, "When you came out here that first time with Jake, I saw how well you two worked together. I wondered if—"

I cut him off sharply. "I'm not involved with Jake."

"There is someone, though, right?"

"Nobody!" I shot back. And without any warning, my eyes filled with tears.

The silence was thick until Paul said, "God, Nora, I'm sorry. You're trying to get over something, aren't you?" Then his strong arms were around me, and I just leaned against him for a minute, wanting the closeness.

He took my bowl of mushrooms, emptied it into his, and said, "Plenty here for an omelette, if you're still willing to have breakfast with me, that is."

"Of course."

As we walked back across the land, I told him a little about Timothy. He listened quietly, reaching out once to touch my hand.

Inside his house, he put on an apron, then gave me some onions and garlic and parsley to chop while he sauteed the mushrooms. He made a superb omelette. Our breakfast conversation was light, impersonal. But walking me to my Jeep he said, "I'm not going to push, Nora, but I'd like to know you better. And you haven't lived until you've tried my stuffed grape leaves."

I laughed, and he smiled. "I'll call you," he said.

A COUPLE OF WEEKS LATER on a morning in early March when skittish clouds couldn't seem to make up their minds to pour down rain or let the sunshine through, Marilyn came to the clinic right after we opened, before Jake had even left on his morning rounds. She seemed relieved to find us all there and accepted Winifred's invitation to share a cup of coffee. Holding the cup tightly, she startled us by announcing that her palomino mare, Purity, was in the last trimester of pregnancy. I hadn't seen a palomino on my visits to her ranch, let alone a mare in foal.

Turning to me, Marilyn explained. "Nora, I've been keeping her in high pasture away from the other mares. She came in heat last spring while I was away working on the referendum. A new rancher across the valley—Jake, I think you know him, Tom Horgan . . ."

Jake nodded.

". . . had been wanting to breed his stud stallion with Purity. He was pretty angry when I told him my ranch was on a breeding moratorium. Well, while I was away he found out Purity was in heat. He and Mel got drunk, and they ended up bringing the stallion over.

"When I got back, Mel was afraid to tell me, so I didn't find out about it until the foal started to show. After what happened with my other mares, I doubted the pregnancy would go full term. But now I'm beginning to think it will. I'd like to make arrangements for Purity to be examined biweekly. Although I'm not sure just when I'd be able to pay you."

Jake's dark eyes were sympathetic as he told Marilyn he'd start including her on his morning rounds.

Startled, I interjected, "But Marilyn is my client."

Winifred set her coffee cup down on the filing cabinet with a sharp little click.

Jake's brow wrinkled, but after a moment he said gruffly, "You're right."

I told Marilyn I'd drive out to her ranch that afternoon, and she said she'd have the mare brought down from high pasture and waiting for me in the barn.

When I got to the ranch, pale sunlight was slanting through the pines onto the weathered barn. Marilyn led me to a stall and then left. Seeing the palomino, I understood why the rancher across the valley had coveted her as a broodmare. She was extraordinary with balanced conformation, strong bones, clean hocks, a beautifully crested neck. Her lips billowed soft warm puffs of air on my shoulders as I palpated her foal; when I looked at her mouth and teeth, she nibbled the hair on my forearms, her limpid eyes blinking complacently when I laughed. After I'd finished, I stroked her champagne-colored coat, so rapt I completely forgot about the threat hanging over her. But when I went to find Marilyn, one look at the anxiety in her eyes was all I needed to remind me.

I said, "Marilyn, she seems *perfect*."

"I know." But there wasn't any conviction in her voice.

"She'll probably foal in late April."

Marilyn nodded. "That's about what I figured." And then, "Nora, if you detect any fetal distress, I want this pregnancy terminated."

I said, "I honestly don't think anything is going to go wrong, but if it does, I'll take care of it."

I asked then if I could take some Polaroid pictures of Purity to send to a friend in the east who needed reminding that creatures like Purity existed.

Marilyn's expression softened as I told her a little about Eileen.

Photographing the animals I cared for was a practice I'd begun during my internship. When children brought in pets whose treatment required long hospital stays, I would take pictures and mail them to the kids with a note about their friend's progress.

I got my Polaroid out of the Jeep, and Marilyn accompanied me to the barn to watch. I swear Purity mugged for the camera. She tossed her head and mane, displaying her beautiful neck to its best advantage.

At home that night, I wrote Eileen a note to go with the photograph: "Her name is Purity, but don't let the name fool you. She's pregnant and flaunting it."

When we talked a week later, Eileen said, "I framed Purity's photograph and put it on my desk next to Nell's sketch. The other lawyers have pictures of husbands, wives, and children. I'm the only one with a horse and a wolf."

She also told me she'd been assigned her first trial case with meat on its bones: a group of Guatemalan pineapple workers were bringing a class-action suit against a U.S. manufacturer of a pesticide. The company had exported the pesticide to Guatemala long after it had been banned in this country.

"Banned for what?" I asked.

"Making workers sterile. A similar suit was filed by Costa Rican banana harvesters a few years ago. The outcome of that one is still pending appeal. I suspect that's why the firm is letting me work on this."

"What do you mean?"

"Their rationale is, they chose me because of my clerkship in the appeals court. But the truth is that they're still afraid of my MS, and they're fairly certain this case will be tied up in the appeals court for years, too."

"How come the plantation owners bought a banned chemical?"

"Profit," she snapped. "The stuff kills nematodes, a worm that feeds on roots. After it was banned in this country, the manufacturer was willing to sell it cheap over there. And, you know, to plantation owners, a dead worm is a hell of a lot more important than a sterile worker." A short silence.

"Oversimplification. That's my problem. I just get so goddamn mad."

"Hey, it's okay," I said. I could tell from the tenor of her voice how keyed up and nervous she was.

"When are you going to put in for some vacation time?" I asked, changing the subject.

"Do I sound that bad? Or do you want some company listening to the trees creak?"

"You've got to take care of yourself," I said firmly.

"Yeah. But you know me, kid. I'm a front-liner, not a hammock type."

Paul called a couple of times in March and again in April, but each time I was on call and had emergencies.

"The luck of the draw," he said ruefully. "I have to make a quick trip to Sacramento for a dairy ranchers' meeting in a week or so. I'll try again when I get back."

PURITY REMAINED IN PEAK CONDITION as her pregnancy progressed, but Marilyn's worry didn't lessen. She waited outside the barn for the results of each examination, her face relaxing only when I announced, "Everything's fine." But when I'd come back two weeks later, the worry would be there again.

By mid-April, Purity's pelvis was relaxed, and the lips of her vulva were swollen and drenched with the beautiful dark rose pre-birth color. After I'd examined her one afternoon, I told Mel to keep a close watch.

Two nights later, Marilyn called to tell me the mare was foaling and to come as quickly as I could. It was a little after 2 a.m.

"Is she having problems?"

"I don't think so. Just come please, Nora."

I hurried into my clothes, and minutes later I was on my way. Despite the anxiety in Marilyn's voice, I was confident Purity was going to birth a normal foal. The sense of urgency I was feeling came from my desire to calm Marilyn—and my own vicarious need to be there, to watch Purity's birth moment.

The night was moonless, and I quickly grew impatient at how slowly I had to negotiate the steep curves on the mountain road. When I got to the ranch, light was spilling out the barn door. Purity lay quietly in the stall I'd instructed Mel to clean and disinfect daily. Nearby were supplies I'd already stocked in the barn and a bucket filled with steaming water. As if she'd been waiting for me, Purity nickered and lifted her head. I knelt and stroked her flanks, glancing quickly at Marilyn. Her auburn hair was loose around her shoulders. The golden light was softening everything except the deep worry lines in her face.

I washed Purity's hindquarters and udder, wrapped her tail, and felt her abdomen to be certain the foal was in the normal position. Scarcely half an hour passed before the outer fetal membrane ruptured and water soaked the floor of the stall. Moments later, the small front hooves appeared, and with a few ripples of effort from Purity, her foal emerged. He was normal—and beautiful. I heard Marilyn's deep sigh and looked up, expecting to see relief. But her expression was still tense as she said, "Examine him carefully, Nora. I'll be in the house."

Watching her disappear through the barn door into the darkness, I caught her worry. Had she seen something I hadn't? Speaking softly to Purity, telling her, "You did your part, lady, all this is just to make sure he's one hundred percent," I examined the foal to be certain he was breathing easily, his nostrils free of any membranes or fluid. He took a hypodermic shot of streptomycin and penicillin with barely a flicker of his eyelashes. I dipped the stump of the umbilical cord in iodine, and moved my fingers slowly, questingly over every inch of his body. Sitting back, I grinned at Purity. "He's wonderful. But you knew that, right?"

I gave Purity a drink of tepid water and some bran mash, and she and I watched her foal work at figuring out what his legs were for. A few minutes later, I left them exploring each other. Walking to the house, looking up at the starlit velvet sky, I felt exuberant.

Marilyn was sitting at her kitchen table with a bottle of brandy and two glasses. She looked up.

"Perfect," I said.

She nodded. "Thanks. I just needed to hear you say it." She poured a finger of brandy into each glass and handed one to me. "To Crusoe."

"Crusoe?"

"That's what I'm going to call him."

I smiled and lifted my glass.

Marilyn said, "Three years ago, I would have had a dozen mares delivering this time of year. Seeing Purity foal made me think—just for a minute—maybe it would be all right again. And then I remembered." She sipped her brandy and tossed her hair back. "Anyhow, we got one, didn't we? And Tom Horgan can eat his heart out."

HALF AN HOUR LATER, I was driving back down Gasquet Mountain. Dawn light seeping through tree branches laid a lacy pattern on the road. Relaxed and happy, my insides warmed by Marilyn's brandy, I had the window open, could smell spring in the air. I was thinking about the words I would use to describe Crusoe's birth to Eileen. Maybe that's why what happened in the next few minutes seemed spun out of a nightmare. I heard a loud roaring sound so completely out of context to my thoughts, I pulled over to the side of the road. The noise grew louder, and I was finally able to match it to a helicopter flying directly toward me.

The nearest airport was two hundred miles away. The only flying machines I'd seen since coming to Combsea had been tiny silver plane specks high in the sky, but this helicopter was flying just above treetop level. Abruptly I understood. The helicopter was spraying Luminex. I rolled up my windows as fast as I could, and as the helicopter passed directly above me, I heard a soft, liquid, pinging sound like tiny raindrops hitting the Jeep's roof. My windshield turned gray. Switching on my wipers until I could see again, I watched the helicopter spray the roadside with a pale mist of the same stuff that glazed my windshield.

The helicopter probably wasn't in my sight or hearing more than five minutes, but it seemed much longer. When it was gone, a sweet, heavy odor seeped through the vents. I made myself drive at a reasonable speed down the winding mountain road, while I tried to quiet my sense of having been attacked. But the sweet stink was nauseating, and as soon as the road straightened, I drove at top speed. Back at my house, I jumped out, peeled off my clothes, and ran for the hose. I turned a strong stream of water on myself and then the Jeep. But merely hosing the stuff off didn't seem like enough. I ran into the house, took a scalding shower, came back out, filled a bucket with water and ammonia and sponged the vehicle with that, hosed it again, went back into the house and showered again. I scrubbed hard, but the stuff still clung to the insides of my nostrils, under my fingernails. Finally I crawled into bed. Burrowing under my quilt, I fell into a deep, exhausted sleep that blotted out the sound of the alarm two hours later.

When I finally woke, half the morning had gone. I'd never been as much as five minutes late to work before. Getting out of bed and dressing as fast as I could, my bones resisted my movements, feeling as if the marrow had turned to lead.

By the time I reached the clinic, Jake was in the middle of handling my appointments. I hurried to get ready to take over, and while I was putting on my white coat, he stuck his head in my office. "You coming down with something?" he said, his eyes concerned.

I told him what had happened on the mountain road.

"Christ!" he exploded. Then, "What were you doing on the mountain at that hour?"

"Purity foaled this morning. I was on my way home from Marilyn's."

His tense expression asked the question.

I said, "Mare and foal are fine."

The tautness around his mouth relaxed for a moment, then came back as he focused on me again. "Look, why don't you go on home? I can handle things here."

I shook my head. Being alone and inactive was the last thing I wanted. I needed to be occupied, and during the next couple of hours, concentrating on animals calmed me. But it didn't dilute my outrage.

Winifred came back to my office during our brief late lunch hour to see how I was doing. She took one look and said, "I'm canceling your afternoon appointments. You should be in bed." She wasn't being sympathetic; just realistic.

I felt awful. I ached all over, and my eyes felt scratchy—perhaps just the symptoms of the onset of a cold induced by the dowsings I'd subjected myself to that morning. But I'd also noticed a red, itchy rash on my arm beginning to form small blisters.

I asked her what she knew about Luminex's effects on people in the valley who'd been briefly exposed.

She didn't meet my eyes. "Pretty much what you've got. Flu-like symptoms. A rash. It's usually mild."

"How long does it last?"

"Varies. Not more than a few days. There don't seem to be any lasting effects, unless . . ." she stopped.

"What?"

"Nothing that would affect you." Then curtly: "I'm sorry about what happened to you, Nora. But you had the spraying schedule, didn't you?"

"Yes."

"So you knew."

I snapped, "I didn't even think about it! Marilyn asked me to come."

"Even though you'd told her you were confident Purity would deliver a normal foal?"

"She was worried."

Winifred's lips formed a thin line.

Despite how awful I felt, I might have taken her on, but we both heard Jake's truck pulling into the parking lot. A minute later, he appeared in the doorway, looked at me, and said, "Nora, get out of here. Now."

I didn't argue.

When I reached home, Marilyn was standing beside her truck in my driveway. As I parked alongside, she hurried to meet me. By then whatever was wrong with me was really taking its toll. Walking hurt.

Marilyn said, "Mel was in town doing some errands and heard what happened."

"How?"

She shrugged. "Combsea's a small town, Nora. Jake took some of your appointments, and Mavis Wilson found out why." Putting a supporting arm around my shoulders, she said, "Let's go inside so you can sit down before you fall down."

As soon as we were inside, all the weariness I'd been damming up broke through. I sank down on the sofa.

Marilyn sat in the chair across from me. "You look awful."

I murmured, "Can't help it."

"I know you can't," she responded. "It's *my* fault."

I shook my head.

But her expression was anguished as she went on, "I had the spraying schedule. I knew they were going to be on the mountain this morning. When Purity started to foal, I just forgot everything else. I'll never be able to make you know how sorry I am."

I told her tiredly I'd had the spraying schedule, too, and hadn't bothered to keep track of it. "Marilyn," I said, "I'm sorry . . . I just . . . I have to sleep. Can't talk any more."

She helped me to the bedroom. I lay down on the bed, and I remember her taking my shoes off, covering me with a blanket, murmuring, "Something has to be done," and that was all.

It was noon the next day when I woke from a dense sleep that had been tossed with nightmares. I'd almost slept the clock around. Feeling disoriented and apprehensive, I got out of bed.

A note from Marilyn was taped to the bathroom mirror: "Fresh orange juice in fridge. Take care of yourself. I'll call you."

I drank a little juice, but I wasn't hungry. I still felt violated. I went outside and stood on my porch, but gazing at the pine trees didn't seem to help. So I got in my Jeep and drove back up Gasquet Mountain, looking for the place I'd encountered the helicopter. I didn't know exactly where it was; my mind had been on the noise, the machine, the spray. But parking in a spot I believed was fairly close, I got out and walked along the roadside.

The manzanita there was dead now, and so was a lot of chaparral. A canyon oak in the spraying path was dying. But the hardest thing for me to absorb was the goshawk I found on the ground. I knelt to stroke its lifeless body, and suddenly I was crying . . . for the hawk, my parents, Timothy. All the grief I'd fought so long not to feel became a stream of pain running through me. I have no idea how long I knelt there, stroking the dead bird and weeping, but the sun was sinking behind the mountain when I finally walked back to the Jeep.

Passing the clinic as I drove through town, I noticed Jake's pick-up was still in the parking lot—no doubt because he'd had to do my work as well as his own for the past two days. I turned in and parked next to his truck.

The light was on in his office and the door was open. I stood looking in.

Jake was seated at his desk, his head bent over an open file. I could tell by the slump of his shoulders how tired he was and I had to resist the impulse I often had to reach out.

"Jake?"

He looked up. "How are you?"

"All right."

He nodded.

I waited, expecting him to say something about the spraying. Nothing.

I asked, "Any major crises here?"

He shrugged. "A steer down with water belly. Otherwise, the usual."

I glanced at the empty chair I'd sat in the day he interviewed me and said, "Can we talk?"

He moved away from the desk a little and flexed his shoulders. "Sure," he said, but his eyes were wary.

I sat down, told him I'd gone back up on the mountain to look at the spraying area, described what I'd seen, and said, "This can't go on."

"Nora, I made it clear where I stood on this issue when I interviewed you."

"Yes," I said, "you did."

"Nothing has changed."

"*I* have."

A deep frown creased his forehead. "Meaning?"

"I can't pretend it isn't happening."

"You don't have to."

"Something has to be done!"

"Not by me." He pushed away from the desk and stood up. "This clinic is not going to become involved in another futile crusade."

He picked up his jacket.

"Jake, wait!"

He shook his head. "I've put in two eighteen-hour days. I'm not going to argue with you, and I'm not going to change my position." He moved toward the door. "Turn out the lights before you leave."

A minute later, I heard his truck pull out of the parking lot. I sat staring at his empty chair for a while listening to the silence.

When I marched out of the clinic, I slammed the door, and left the lights on.

BY THE END OF THE WEEK, the flu-like ache, fatigue, and rash had disappeared, but rage about Luminex had become a filament running through my nights and days. I certainly felt its presence whenever Jake and I were together. Our Friday after-work conferences were strained now. Tension was building.

Then when I was reading the weekly paper over dinner one evening, a notice of the monthly Combsea Town Council meeting brought to mind a town meeting I'd attended once with Nell. I'd been a resistant, opinionated adolescent at the time and hadn't wanted to go, but Nell insisted. She'd said it was part of my education.

The subject at issue in Nell's Santa Monica neighborhood had been the spill-over of untreated sewage into the ocean after heavy storms. Nell told me I might see a few normally reasonable people become foul-tempered, maybe even go a little berserk in their zeal to end contamination of the beaches, and that's exactly what happened. One elderly gentleman walked up onto the stage carrying a shoebox, and when he reached the podium, took the lid off and lifted out the body of a gull whose wings were caked with brown, evil-smelling sludge.

The man stood for a minute, gazing out at us before he said, "You know, I don't like gulls. Never have. They're scavengers, like wharf rats. But this . . . I wouldn't inflict it on a rat or a gull or any other living creature. I know it's going to cost us time, effort, and *money* to clean up the mess we've made. And a lot of people would rather put up with the mess than spend the money. They think it's not going to make one iota of difference in their lives if every gull disappears from the earth. But, you see, the putrefaction on the gull's wings is in the ocean, and one day it will *be* the ocean."

Entering the clinic the next morning, what was on my mind was on my face. Winifred came to the door of my office soon after Jake had left, her features set in the expression I'd seen when she talked to clients who could afford to pay their bills and didn't. She said tersely, "Stop judging Jake. You don't know enough."

I said, "I'm not judging him."

"The hell you're not," she snapped.

And she was gone.

I stared at the empty doorway. *Was* I judging Jake—or myself—or both of us?

Half an hour later, Winifred buzzed the intercom to tell me an emergency call had come from Briervale. I was really surprised. Arnold Brier's cattle ranch, the largest in the valley, was Jake's client, but Winifred said she hadn't been able to reach Jake on the shortwave. Since that had never happened before, I got the feeling she was putting me through some kind of test, and I wasn't in a mood to walk away.

Briervale sprawled over hundreds of acres of flat, leased rangeland. When I got to the ranch headquarters, the foreman led me around to a small back birthing pasture where a cow had gone into labor prematurely and her calf had breeched. There hadn't been time to get the animal into a birthing chute. While the foreman talked to her softly, I reached up into the birth canal to reposition the calf and secure a grip-chain around its legs, sensing even as I did so, that something was terribly wrong. I pulled the calf out. It was blind and deformed, its spine twisted and its testicles atrophied.

For a moment, shock deadened emotion.

I was aware of the foreman watching me.

He asked, "This your first one?"

I nodded.

"Probably won't be your last."

Then his eyes slid away from the calf, and he mumbled he'd go get the owner. I gave the mother a tranquilizer, held the misshapen creature in my arms, and waited. It made little mewling sounds, and its heart-beat was erratic. Was it in pain? How could I know?

Almost twenty minutes passed before the foreman returned with Arnold Brier. He was younger than I'd expected; probably in his mid-thirties. He had light brown hair and cool gray eyes. A woman I judged to be Mrs. Brier followed a few steps behind her husband. She was pale and fragile-looking and averted her eyes from the creature in my lap.

I expected Arnold Brier to be upset about the calf, from a mone-tary standpoint if nothing else. But he only glanced at it briefly and said, "Where's Jake?"

"On another call."

"You can go ahead and kill it."

As he started to walk away, I asked, "How often does this happen?"

He turned. His eyes narrowed. "You know anything about what broadleaf weeds can do to rangeland, Miss?"

"*Doctor.* Yes, I do."

"So you've seen ripgut, filaree, and mouse barley?"

"I know what they are," I replied. "They're weeds that take over rangeland after the grasses are thinned by overgrazing."

"Or drought or blight or bad weather or any other number of damn things. You ever treat an animal with grass tetany from eating those kinds of weeds?"

"Yes."

His eyes flicked the creature in my arms. "They were a hell of a lot worse off than that calf, weren't they?"

"They were in pain. But we could save them. They were going to live."

He ignored that. "I suppose you've seen herds of underfed cattle, too."

"No."

"God and the chemical companies willing, you won't have to. We have good healthy rangeland now because the weeds that used to choke out our grazing grasses are killed by Luminex."

"Luminex kills lots of things. And there are other ways to kill weeds."

"Yeah? You know anything about profit margins in raising cattle?"

"Not much."

"Around here, we like to winter pasture our cattle. And with our weed-free rangeland, we can deliver fat healthy animals to the feed lots in the spring and make a big enough profit to keep our ranches and families going."

"At what price?"

"At *no* price compared to what it used to be. I remember how it was during bad years for my dad, and I am not going back to that!" He stopped, drew in a breath, and let it out slowly, then said, "Maybe you heard how—a couple of years ago—me and my friends got a little upset about the referendum certain people in this valley were trying to get on the ballot."

"I heard."

"Well, referendums can be tricky, so we decided to put a stop to it, and we did. Cost us some money but nothing we couldn't afford.

"Then when we found out Jake had got himself an associate from Berkeley, we wondered whether we were going to have some more trouble. So we contacted certain people in Sacramento, and they called other people in Washington. And you know what we found out? We don't have a goddamn thing to worry about. We've dotted every 'i' and crossed every 't,' and the law is on our side. You keep asking the wrong kinds of questions, all you'll do is make trouble for Jake and other folks around here who can't afford trouble.

"Now, you want to know how many deformed calves I've had, you check Jake's files at the clinic. But I'll tell you something. There isn't a damn thing you can do with that information once you get it. How I bear my losses is up to me." He started to leave the pasture, but turned back. "I want Jake taking *all* the calls from this ranch from now on." Then he did leave. After a quick, agonized gaze at the animal in my lap, his wife followed.

I gave the calf the euthanasia injection, holding it in my arms until it stopped breathing. Then I wrapped it in a tarp and laid it in the back of my Jeep. As I climbed up into the driver's seat, I saw the foreman kneel beside the mother cow to hold her head. She was struggling to get up, lowing softly for her calf.

Driving back to Combsea, I clenched the steering wheel, taking the curves a little too fast, trying to convince myself that even though I'd disliked Arnold Brier and didn't agree with a thing he'd said, that didn't necessarily make him wrong or me right. He was a cattle rancher, and his eye was on the herd, not one calf, just as Will Jenkins's had been on the yield of trees. The problem was we weren't talking about replacing warped bolts on an assembly line. We were talking about living things. And I remembered something Eileen had said more than once: "The law can be a real slow learner."

On sudden impulse, instead of turning back toward town, I took the mountain road up to Marilyn's. I'd been wanting to talk to her ever since my conversation with Jake, and even more now, after my clash with Arnold Brier.

Half an hour later, I parked in Marilyn's driveway and sat in the Jeep trying to organize my thoughts before I got out. Purity and Crusoe were in the paddock. The bright April sunlight burnished their coats. I stood leaning on the fence speaking to them softly, soaking up their beauty.

Hearing my voice, Marilyn came out of the barn. Bits of straw clung to her auburn braids. Brushing them away, she leaned on the paddock rail next to me. "Well, you look better than you did the last time I saw you."

"I do, huh," I said testily.

She caught the flush of anger on my cheekbones and asked, "How are you really?"

"Physically I'm okay. But I need to talk."

She nodded. "Go ahead."

I told her about Jake's and my being at such odds. "I've just come from the Brier ranch. One of their cows had a breech birth. It's in the back of my Jeep."

Her face flinched at the pronoun, but she didn't comment.

"I'm going back to the clinic and take some Polaroid pictures of that calf to pass around at the town council meeting on Wednesday. While people are looking at those pictures, I'm going to explain what verdicides do to embryos. I'd like you to come with me."

I'd been so positive she would say yes that I was stunned when she said, "It would be useless for either of us to go to that meeting."

"How could anyone look at pictures of what's in my Jeep and not be affected?" I demanded.

"Arnold Brier wasn't, was he? And he's on the town council, Nora. The rest of the members think just like he does. Otherwise, they wouldn't be on the council. Everyone who fought this issue was beaten by those people. You've just helped a cow give birth to a deformed calf, and I know the agony you're feeling better than anyone. But what you're planning is futile."

"Is your moratorium futile?"

"I didn't start my moratorium to accomplish anything politically. I did it because I couldn't breed my horses when I knew what their foals might be like. So, no, it isn't futile."

"Well, okay. But that afternoon you came to my house after the spraying, you said something had to be done."

"I know. And after I left and you were so sick and I felt responsible, I couldn't sleep. So I called an old friend, another breeder who lives in a spraying region in Oregon. I told her about my moratorium and some of the things I'd been reading and thinking, and she listened. Then she called a friend and that friend called a friend and a kind of chain began to form. We've all begun keeping written records of what has happened wherever Luminex is used. A few of the other breeders are initiating moratoriums, too. I don't know where it's going to lead us, whether what Martin Luther King called 'unarmed truth' can actually work. But it's a place to begin."

"Then why not give it a test," I urged. "Come to the meeting with me. Talk to them the way you're talking to me right now."

"Anybody who would listen to me won't be there."

"Well, but people can't just give up," I said, adding sullenly, "like Jake." I gave one of the paddock support posts an angry kick, startling Purity's foal into a beautiful coltish gallop. Marilyn and I watched in silence, and then Marilyn spoke quietly.

"At considerable risk, Jake supported the referendum."

For a moment, I was too surprised to speak. "He didn't tell me that."

"No, he wouldn't."

"I gather you've known each other a long time."

"We went through school together. He's a good man, Nora."

"I know he is. He's the most gentle, compassionate veterinarian I've ever worked with. That's why I don't understand how he can go on ignoring what Luminex does to the animals he treats."

"He isn't ignoring it."

"Then what is he doing? Putting up with it? Damn it, he's going to have to take a stand!"

I gazed into the paddock, struggling with the realization that I was condemning Jake for the same things Eileen used to challenge in me —passivity and retreat.

Finally I turned to leave, mumbling, "I have to get back to the clinic." But near my Jeep, I stopped and turned. " 'Unarmed truth' takes too long. Come with me," I pleaded.

She shook her head.

"Well, I'm going," I said. "And what's more, I'll make them listen."

"God knows, I wish you luck."

At the clinic, I carried the calf into my examining room and laid it on the table. Then I went into the supply room, opened a drawer of Winifred's filing cabinet, pulled out the Briervale file, and scanned it. Since February, seven cows in Arnold Brier's herd had delivered deformed calves. I shut the drawer with a bang and went to Winifred's office.

She was working at the computer but stopped.

"Has Jake been treating *all* the clients whose animals have been affected by Luminex since I got here?" I asked.

"Yes. Except for Marilyn." She pushed away from her desk irritably. "I told him he shouldn't turn the O'Hare ranch over to you. But he said because Marilyn wasn't breeding her horses, you wouldn't have any problem. *I* knew there'd be trouble. Marilyn carries a big chip on her shoulder."

"What breeder wouldn't whose foals were murdered!" I snapped. Then I tried to calm down. "Jake had no right to keep all this from me."

"Depends on how you look at it. I gather you and Arnold had quite a talk."

"How do you know?"

"He called. He doesn't want you going out there again."

"And that's what you wanted to happen?"

"I wanted to get this mess out in the open."

"What mess? Damn it, what's going on?"

"About a month after you started working here, a group of timber-men and cattle ranchers came to see Jake late one afternoon. You were out. They may even have arranged that. Anyway, on a surface level, their faces were friendly, but it was a look that goes with being in power.

"I'm not ashamed to say I eavesdropped. I heard those men tell Jake they hadn't been too worried about his supporting the referendum because they knew they could stop it from passing. On the other hand, they hadn't liked his supporting it. They didn't want people getting all riled up *again* because some Berkeley radical was running around stirring things up. If it looked like that was going to happen, they would hire themselves some vets and set up their own clinic."

"Then that's why he's been taking all their calls?"

"Exactly."

I started to say something, but she held up a restraining hand. "Jake knew he was taking a risk when he hired you. He did it because he could tell you were going to be every bit as good a vet as you've turned out to be, and he trusted you when you told him you wouldn't try and change things. What I want to know is, why did you lie?"

Her question hit me hard. It took a minute before I could speak. "I wasn't lying. I just didn't know how the spraying would affect me."

"Now that you do, maybe you ought to leave."

My hands clenched. "The only person who has the right to say that to me is Jake."

"Well, you keep pushing him, and I expect he will. Right now he figures he got himself into this mess so he'll get himself out. But he's wearing himself thin trying to protect you *and* the clinic. You don't have the right to place him under that kind of stress. You don't even belong here."

"Take a look at what's on my examining table, and then you tell me who and what belongs here!" Trembling, I spun around and walked back down the corridor to my examining room, went in, shut the door and then leaned against it with my eyes closed. I needed to cool down so I could think.

But opening my eyes, the first thing I saw was the dead creature on my examining table. What was there to *think* about?

I took my Polaroid out of the cupboard and used up all the film I had left. I was still holding the camera when there was a knock on the door and Jake opened it.

"You didn't hear me say, 'Come in,' " I said sharply.

He stood in the doorway, his eyes moving from the calf to the camera to me. "Winifred told me where you'd been today and what happened."

I nodded.

"What are you going to do with those pictures?"

"I'm going to the town council meeting."

He ran his fingers through his hair. "Nora, don't."

He looked so depressed and exhausted, I wished I could say something kind. Instead I said, meaning it, "I'm sorry. I have to go to that meeting."

WEDNESDAY NIGHT, driving to the high school auditorium where the town council met, I was scared and nervous. If this was how Eileen felt when she went into a courtroom the first few times, it was no wonder she used a wheelchair.

Earlier that week, I'd gone through the clinic files in the supply room, compiling a case count of animals born deformed and put to death. I'd tried to do it when Winifred was most apt to be busy in her office, but one morning she came in while I was taking notes. Moving close enough to glance into the file drawer, she wanted to know, "Why are you looking at Jake's files?"

"Just checking something," I said, and shut the drawer. By then, I'd gotten what I needed. I was about halfway down the hall to my office when I heard her open the drawer. Assuming she was going to try and figure out what I'd been up to and reluctantly acknowledging her stubborn perseverance, I'd wished tiredly that we could be allies instead of adversaries. And that night, driving past Jake's house on the edge of town, I felt a similar mix of sadness and resentment that he wasn't going to the meeting with me.

There weren't many cars in the high school parking lot. When I walked into the auditorium and looked around, I didn't know whether to be relieved or disappointed at how few people were there. I took a seat in the second row on a hard metal chair just like ones I'd sat on during assemblies at Santa Monica High. Henry Mahler was sitting in the front row, and we exchanged quick smiles. Scanning the faces of the people at the council table on stage, I saw three men, including Arnold Brier, and two women. One was a Mrs. Mason whose collie I'd treated for mange a month earlier. Her young son had been curious about the instruments he'd seen inside my cabinet, and asked what I was looking for when I examined their collie. Mrs. Mason had said tautly, "Lon, you just keep your lips zipped and let the lady do her work." She acknowledged my presence now with a slight nod.

Perhaps twenty people were seated by the time the meeting was called to order. We listened while the minutes of the previous meeting were read and pending matters on the agenda were dealt with—after which the chairman announced that the floor was open for new business.

Henry immediately stood up and was given the floor. He stated that the clock above the bank on Combsea's main street ought to be set and kept at the correct time. In the spring, when daylight savings time went into effect, Combsea's sole clock repairman often took three months to move the hands on the clock forward, and when the time switched to standard, three more months to move them back. Even when the clock was set at the right hour, he continued, the minutes were generally off. Henry displayed a paper with signatures of townspeople who agreed with him. Apparently it was an issue that had been broached before, because the ensuing discussion quickly narrowed to the age of the clock's mechanism, the skill (or lack of it) of the repairman, and whether someone should be brought over from Clarksville. I admired Henry's persistence and hoped he might be an ally when I presented my issue.

The second item of new business involved the expansion of a gas station at the edge of town. I didn't listen, focusing instead on my resolve to speak next.

When the gas station discussion ended, I raised my hand and the chairman granted me the floor. I mounted the short flight of steps to the stage, handed the chairman four of the Polaroid pictures of the dead calf, asked him to pass them around, returned to my place, and distributed the remaining pictures among people in the audience. I kept my hands clenched to hide their shaking. While the pictures were changing hands, I talked about the number of animals I knew about that had delivered deformed newborns during the past year. Then I made a motion that the spraying be suspended in Clark County while an in-depth study of Luminex's effects on human beings and animals was undertaken.

The reactions I got ranged from an embarrassed, foot-shifting silence among people in the audience, to studied indifference or annoyance from most of the council members. From Arnold Brier there was a thin, self-satisfied smile. Mrs. Mason, whose concern for the well-being of her collie was all any veterinarian could wish for, didn't look at me. I glanced quickly across at Henry Mahler. He was studying his knees.

The chairman asked if anyone cared to comment. No one did. He asked if there was a second to my motion. There was not.

I couldn't believe I hadn't reached a single person.

I said, "Mrs. Mason, what if I'd passed around pictures of a deformed collie pup?"

She gave no sign she'd heard me.

The chairman cleared his throat and let a moment of silence pass before he said, "We'll go on to the next topic if there is no further comment." There wasn't. Someone in the row behind me stood up, was acknowledged and given the floor, but I didn't hear a word that was said. For the sake of my pride, I didn't leave until the meeting adjourned, but I knew from past experience how my face was revealing my emotions.

Finally, it was over. I hurried to reach the sheltering darkness outside and was the first one to drive out of the parking lot. Going down Main Street, brushing away angry tears, I remembered something Eileen had said one evening in the Benvenue house. After she'd spent weeks looking for a group home for a mentally disabled man living on the streets, he'd refused to move in. He preferred what he called, "the freedom of the streets." She'd said, "People's psyches are labyrinths. It's amazing how they seldom do what you think they will—and how much that teaches you about your own expectations."

Nearing Jake's house, I noticed the lights were still on. I pulled over to the curb, parked, and sat for a while, staring at the front door.

Finally I got out of the Jeep, walked up, and rang the bell.

I heard a whoompfing bark, and when Jake opened the door, an elderly basset hound stuck his nose out to sniff my knees. I knelt and stroked the soft ears and velvety coat.

Jake's eyes were wary, but his tone was noncommittal as he said, "Meet Magruder, though it's plain he feels like he already knows you." Then, "What's up?"

"Can I come in?"

"Sure."

Magruder's tail thumped a welcome as I entered the house, which I could see right away belonged to a man who didn't really live in it. It wasn't unkempt, but I got the feeling that the living and dining rooms Jake led me past on the way to the kitchen were rooms the two of them rarely used.

I smelled something cooking, guessed I'd caught Jake in the middle of a late dinner, and wondered what kind of meals he prepared for himself. Despite how well I knew him as a veterinarian, his life away from the clinic was a mystery.

An empty clam chowder can was on the counter top in the kitchen, its half-eaten contents in a bowl on the table next to a plate of salad.

Jake sat down, gesturing for me to do the same.

I did and Magruder lay at my feet, resting his bony head on my shoe.

Silence hung between us like a bat on the rafters. Finally Jake asked, "How did it go?"

"If you'd been there," I said, "you would have seen me make a fool of myself."

He pushed back from the table. "I imagine I'll have other chances."

Left-over anger and frustration rose to the surface. "Part of the reason it went badly is because I was alone. No one in this valley— including you—seems to give a damn."

He stood up. " 'Give a damn!' About what, Nora? The town, the people, the animals in my care? My god, who do you think you are? You've been here—what—eight months, and you're telling me I don't give a damn?"

I swallowed and said, "I'm sorry. You got some of the anger I should have let out at the meeting. I know how it must pain you when an animal is harmed by the spraying. And I also know about those men who came to see you. Winifred told me."

He nodded.

"But if you keep accepting the spraying, accommodate it by remaining silent, the things you love will be eroded."

He shook his head. "No, they won't."

I was dumbfounded. "Can't you *hear* me?"

"Nora—"

I cut him off. "So you can actually stand there and tell me it's all right for people in this valley to accept the use of a substance that deforms fetuses?"

"No," Jake said, "I can't. But it's not a simple choice between right and wrong. A lot of people in this valley depend on companies that support the spraying. They accept it because they're afraid of what will happen if they don't."

"What about you? Are you afraid?"

"I'm not going to lose my clinic, Nora."

"That's why you accept it?"

"I live with it. And I provide the best veterinary care I know how to. Which is what you told me you were going to do."

"And I am. But how do you provide good veterinary care to a calf born blind and without testicles?"

His lips tightened. "You euthanize and handle it just as you would any other animal's death."

"Even though you know that death didn't have to happen?"

Jake picked up his salad plate, carried it to the sink, put it down sharply and turned to face me. "Stop it."

"Stop what? Trying to figure out how to put an end to what's happening in Combsea?"

"Yes! Christ. Winifred's right. You don't belong here."

I just stared at him. How could we be at such loggerheads when his passion for protecting animals was as intense as mine?

The effort he was making to control his temper was visible. He said, "Look, I've been giving this situation a lot of thought ever since the other night at the clinic. I believe your exposure to Luminex is making you react in ways you wouldn't have before."

"Damn right! But that's not the only thing. Marilyn's barren horses, Arnold Brier's calf, the deformed animal births in your files, the goshawk I found, the dead trees . . . my god!"

"That's all you can see now, isn't it? When you first came here, you could see the town, its way of life. You said you wanted that. I thought you did. Now all you can see is Luminex."

I heard something final in his voice.

"What are you saying?"

"I knew you wouldn't accomplish anything at the town meeting. I hoped it would convince you to stop what you're doing. But it didn't."

"No," I agreed. "So?"

"I believe it's time for you to use the separation clause. I'll reimburse you for the expense of your move up here and write you the best letter of recommendation I know how. That way, you shouldn't have any trouble obtaining a position at another clinic."

" 'Another clinic,' " I echoed.

"Yes."

Fury shot through me. "To hell with your letter! The day you offered me the associateship, you asked if I could accept animals born deformed. My answer was, I didn't know. Well, now I know I can't accept it. But that doesn't affect my ability as a veterinarian. *You* can use the damned separation clause if you want to, but if you do, I'll fight you. Even if I know I'm going to lose. And it'll be a battle you won't forget!"

A second later, I was out the door.

WHEN I GOT HOME, the phone was ringing as I walked up my porch steps. I glanced at my watch. Eileen must be burning the midnight oil again. My mood was so foul I debated whether to answer it —but I did.

It was Paul.

"I've been calling for days," he said. "Where have you been?"

"Busy!" I snapped.

"Sounds like I picked a good time to call."

"I'm sorry. I'm exhausted, Paul. Let me call you tomorrow."

I replaced the receiver and a second later, it rang again. I picked it up just to stop the ringing and heard Eileen's voice. "Nora? You there?"

I sighed. "Yeah, I'm here.

"You just get home?"

"Uh-huh."

"Did you have an emergency?"

"No."

"I thought they rolled up the sidewalks at eight o'clock."

"Yes, well . . ."

"You sound exhausted. What's going on?"

Suddenly I was so hungry to be with her face-to-face that I poured it all out—telling her about Luminex, the defeated referendum, Marilyn's horses, Arnold Brier's calf, the town meeting.

"My god!" she said. "You actually went to the meeting and stood up to those people?"

"I don't know if 'stood up' describes what I did."

"But you went. You spoke."

"Yeah," I agreed, remembering I hadn't told her about my exposure to the spraying or Jake's attitude.

"Tell me exactly what happened at that meeting."

After I had, she was silent for several moments. Then: "Your tactics were wrong."

I felt completely drained and her statement stung. "Gee, thanks."

"Nora, you talked to those people about deformed animal births. But that's the effect, not the cause. People—especially scared people—rationalize. They say, 'Too bad about Arnold Brier's calf, but he can afford the loss, and him losing a calf isn't going to affect me.' " She paused a second. "How about I put my thinking cap on?"

I was still irritated. "What for?"

"Maybe I'll come up with something."

"Like what?"

"Information, Nora. That's usually a good place to start. And the research consultant we use is a whiz. It won't take him long to find out everything there is to know about Luminex."

I told her to go ahead, but after we said goodbye, I sat staring out my window quite a while. Gathering information was one thing, but if she were actually to get involved . . . well, I was too tired to think about it. Besides, how could she?

WHAT I HAD DONE sifted through the town.

Most people's reactions were probably mild because I hadn't accomplished anything.

Actually, there was one change: I became completely invisible to the people I'd been *almost* invisible to before.

Paul called to ask if I was all right. I said I was. He said, "Okay." That was it.

The first time I saw Henry Mahler, he started to cross the street—

I assumed to avoid talking to me—then changed his mind and came back and asked the usual question, "How's my cabin treating you?"

"Fine."

His faded eyes looked sad. "Wouldn't have done any good if any of us had stood up for you," he said. "They've got the power." Then he patted my shoulder. "You carry on."

I thought Zelda seemed solicitous when I went into the bakery then decided that was my imagination. But as I was leaving, she said, "Nora?"

I turned. "Hm?"

"My husband Ray said, what you did took spunk."

After a second I answered, "Thank him for me, will you?"

She nodded.

The day I went to get my honey jars refilled, Mavis Wilson was more direct than anyone. She said, "You can't mess around like that if you want to keep on working here. Shoot, Nora, I lose some of my bees after every spraying. But I know better than to make a fuss about it." Ladling the honey in, she went on, "If you were just living here, that might be different, maybe you could say what you wanted. But people in this town care about Jake. What you do could affect him, and he's had trouble enough."

"What kind of trouble?"

Screwing my jar lids on, she gave me a sidelong glance, "Why don't I make us a cup of tea?"

While we were drinking our tea, she told me how Jake's life had changed after his brother, Les, was killed in Vietnam. Les was ten years older and a lot more serious than Jake, and the two had never been especially close. That's why everybody was so surprised when they found out Les had named Jake his beneficiary on his serviceman's life insurance policy.

"Before that happened, Jake was real fun-loving. I remember on his high school graduation night, he and some of his buddies went up Gasquet Mountain and rode down one of the logging flumes in their birthday suits." Mavis smiled at the memory. "Could have broken their fool necks." She sighed. "Anyhow, after Les died and Jake got the insurance money, it was almost like he believed Les was telling him to get busy and do something with his life. He used the money to go to college . . . San Luis Obispo, then Davis . . . but he would come home a couple times a month—to see Jennifer."

Her mouth pursed a little bit, as if what she were saying had taken on a bitter taste. "Jennifer was Jake's sweetheart all the way through grammar and high school. I don't know, if Jake hadn't changed so much, stayed easy going and all, maybe things would have worked out. But he got so duty bound. Everybody could see Jennifer wasn't enjoying that much, and while he was away at college she did a lot of running around. But she married him when he finished at Davis. Probably she thought he'd get back to being his old self. And being a veterinarian's wife sure beat marrying one of the loggers she'd been carrying on with.

"Thing was, Jake had to spend every cent he had left to get the clinic going, so he and Jennifer moved in with his parents. And they were old, you know." Mavis shook her head. "One Fourth of July weekend . . . I guess Jennifer and Jake had been married about two years . . . Jennifer just packed up her things and ran off with a tractor salesman. She sent Jake the divorce papers six months later. Rumor has it, she didn't stay with the tractor salesman either. Last anybody heard of her, she was down in San Diego."

She looked up from her teacup. "But it's like little slippages have taken place inside Jake, and he can't get himself back. After his parents died, he dated a school teacher who lived in Clarksville for a while, but nothing ever came of it. Most folks think it was kind of a double whammy—his brother and then what Jennifer did. That's why he works so hard."

Well, that I could understand.

FINDING OUT ABOUT JAKE'S LIFE helped explain the darkness I'd kept glimpsing. But it didn't change what I thought about Luminex—or the fact that I believed his "living with it" was wrong.

Every day, I expected an envelope from his attorney to show up— but it didn't.

Then one Saturday, we both had to work on a sheep ranch at the far end of the valley. It was the first time we'd worked together since I'd taken over my share of the clients.

The owners of the ranch, the Etchamendys, were a close-knit Basque family. They all pitched in that afternoon—husband, wife, sons, daughters, nieces, nephews. Their flock was afflicted with mite mange, and each sheep had to be doused with a strong antiseptic dip. It was hot, exhausting work, partly because we all wore hooded slickers that covered us from head to toe.

We finished about four o'clock in the afternoon. Jake and the men went to the barn shower to wash, and I accepted Mrs. Etchamendy's invitation to clean up in the bathroom in the main house.

When I came out into the kitchen, her table was laden with Basque food: potato soup, pickled tongue, Pyrenees bread, lamb stew. She insisted Jake and I stay for supper. Everyone was drinking Picon punch, which I'd heard of but never tasted. Mr. Etchamendy offered me a cup, and it tasted wonderful, a heady blend of brandy, grenadine, soda, and Amer Picon aperitif. He kept refilling my cup whenever it reached the half-empty point.

After supper, the oldest Etchamendy son—a young man with eyes like midnight and skin the color of clover honey—brought out his fiddle and played while his younger sister sang a Basque love song in a lilting soprano. I glanced over at Jake once, and he was listening intently, his sad eyes never leaving the young woman's face. Then the fiddler upped the tempo, and two of the men started twirling their wives around, and the young woman who'd sung the love song invited Jake to dance with her. As he spun her around, he laughed out loud once and the years slipped away from his face, and I could see the young man he must have been. When that song ended he came over and held out his hand. I hesitated, not sure how well I could dance in boots, but he just pulled me to my feet. We danced so fast, I got dizzy.

After a while, everybody was too tired to dance any more, and the fiddler put away his instrument.

I was the first to leave. As I started to pick up the jacket I'd left on the back of a chair, Jake picked it up first. Holding the jacket for me, his hand brushed my cheek. Silence as thick as a fur pelt followed that brief touch. Then Mr. Etchemendy said something, and Jake turned to answer him.

Walking out to the Jeep, I was tired, full of good food, mellowed by the Picon punch and the music. I carried a loaf of bread Mrs. Etchamendy had insisted I take, after she told me shyly I should eat more. The sheep were lowing, I could smell alfalfa, the mountains in the distance were the color of licorice. I stood still for a minute, in the midst of it.

Jake, behind me, said, "Nora?"

I was so startled I jumped, and dropped my package. We both knelt to pick it up, and our heads almost bumped. Jake smiled. I noticed that he was holding a small jug. "Picon punch. The Etchamendys never let anybody go away empty-handed."

We started walking slowly toward the parking area and Jake said, "Seems to me there's a lot worth saving, Nora, if we could just get past this Luminex thing."

I murmured, "I know."

"Maybe we should talk some more."

"Maybe."

Watching him cross the yard to his pick-up, the tiredness in his movements made him seem vulnerable, stirring that wanting-to-reach-out feeling again. Or maybe it was the things Mavis Wilson had told me. Or just having seen him laugh and have a good time.

When he reached his truck, he turned. "Will you follow me home?"

I hesitated, but nodded.

His truck's red taillights were like illuminated magnets pulling me along the road. But by the time we got to his house, I was having second thoughts. I pulled up behind him but didn't get out.

Jake walked back to my window. "Change your mind?"

"I don't know."

"Thing is, Magruder liked the way you scratched his ears. I'll build a fire . . . and we can have a last cup of Picon punch and talk. We don't have to settle anything tonight." His eyes wouldn't let go of mine.

He turned away, and I watched him walk up his front porch steps.

As he opened his door, I heard Magruder's hoarse, welcoming bark. Jake called, "He wants to know if you're coming."

Slowly, I got out and followed.

As soon as I was inside, Magruder licked my ankles, sniffed my aroma to see if any of it had changed since my last visit, then went to lie beside the hearth and watch Jake put logs and kindling in the fireplace. The soft thumping of Magruder's tail registered his approval of all of us being in this unused room. I sat down on the couch to watch, too. It was a well-laid fire, and when Jake put a match to it, it flared up fast. While the kindling was still in the snapping stage, he went out to the kitchen and returned with two glasses of Picon punch. The reddish amber color looked wonderful in the firelight.

We sat on the couch staring into the flames. After what seemed a long time, Jake reached over and took my hand.

If I hadn't wanted that to happen, I wouldn't have been sitting next to him.

He just held my hand for a while, and I closed my eyes, thinking about all the times I'd watched his hands, marveling at their gentleness, realizing that for a long, long time, I'd wanted them touching me. He pulled me to my feet, and I followed him up the stairs to his room. We undressed each other slowly, and then we were making love, the loneliness and pain marooned in each of us reaching out for rescue.

We fell asleep in each other's arms, and I woke to find him brushing each of my fingers with his lips, and then his tongue. I pulled my hand away so nothing would be between his mouth and mine, and when our lips opened to each other, all the need and hunger were there again.

Jake was still asleep when I left his house. I drove home in my Jeep, watching the sun light the mountain tops. Then it disappeared behind a cloud moving across the sky.

OVER THE NEXT FEW DAYS, I was acutely aware of the smell of Jake's sweat after he'd been out in the field, the scent of sage and

eucalyptus he brought into the clinic, and the texture of his clothes—
the worn places in his jeans on the knees and buttocks, the soft
flannel of his shirts, the fleecy lining of his jacket. For a while his arms
fascinated me; then it was the line of his profile against the light.

Wednesday evening, we came out of our offices into the corridor at
precisely the same moment. We both stopped and stood absolutely
still—like kids playing a game of statues.

Jake said, "Had dinner yet?"

"No."

"Want to join me and the hound?"

"Oh, yes."

So home with him I went.

We made time for each other after that. Usually I'd follow him to
his house after our clinic conference on Friday, and we'd make love as
desperately as if we believed our world were coming to an end, ignoring
—though I knew it couldn't remain ignored—Luminex. Our bodies
(and souls, too, I suppose) were so starved for company and comfort,
we just surrendered to that.

One Friday evening, instead of following Jake home the way I
usually did, I drove to my house to shower and put on the dress Nell
had given me. Removing the barrette that held my hair away from my
face, I brushed my hair, then let it fall loosely on my shoulders. Looking
at myself for a long time in the only mirror in the house, an old
cloudy one on the back of the door in the bathroom, I didn't recognize
the young woman who stared back at me.

Driving to Jake's, the touch of soft fabric on my bare legs made me
feel unfamiliar to myself. So did my hair blowing about my face.
When I reached his house, I stood on the porch for a minute before I
knocked.

Jake opened the door and light from inside the house streamed out.
He backed away a little and stood staring at me. "God, Nora, you
look . . . you look lovely." He reached for my hand, drew me inside,
then abruptly seemed shy.

I went to stand in front of the fireplace until Magruder, who didn't
give a damn what I had on or how I wore my hair, came and snuffled

his way up under my skirt as close to my crotch as a basset's short legs would reach. I started to laugh. Jake came over to join us then, and I reached out to him, and pretty soon the dress was off, and we were upstairs in his big old feather bed.

I didn't go home that night. Saturday morning we got up and cooked breakfast together. Or, rather, he cooked and I ate. Just as we were finishing, the telephone rang.

Jake picked it up. "Yes?" Silence. "I'll be right there." He hung up.

His expression was grim.

"Jake?"

"Two horses with EIA. On the Dakin ranch."

Our eyes held.

Equine infectious anemia is one of the most dreaded of all horse diseases; there are no protective immunities. It's fatal and spreads quickly. Because an animal can be a carrier without showing any symptoms, the law requires equine owners to have their horses blood-tested yearly. If a horse tests positive, it has to be put down.

I'd asked to put down an EIA-infected horse during my internship so I would know I could do it, and I hadn't forgotten that experience.

I said, "I'll go with you."

I put on an old pair of Jake's jeans and one of his shirts, and a few minutes later we were in his pick-up on the way to the Dakin ranch.

Mr. Dakin was standing in front of his ranchhouse when we got there. He led us out to a field where his hired hands were preparing a deep hole with a bulldozer. One of the horses to be put down turned out to be Mrs. Dakin's riding horse, a handsome bay. The woman stood silently holding the bay's halter, tears streaming down her face.

Moving swiftly, speaking softly and soothingly, Jake injected the lethal solution into the bay's neck. A few seconds later, the horse staggered and collapsed. Mrs. Dakin quickly left the pasture. While Mr. Dakin and his helpers pulled the dead animal into the hole—which kept filling up with mud and water from an underground spring—Jake moved to inject the second horse.

After it was over and Jake and I were walking back to the pick-up, I felt powerless, defeated, the same kind of feeling I got about Eileen's

MS. Which is probably why I said, "At least a helicopter didn't fly over those animals spraying them with it," as I climbed into the pick-up.

It was the first time I'd mentioned Luminex since our argument the night of the town meeting. Jake's lips tightened, and his hands clenched the steering wheel. He was silent all the way back to his house.

By the time we got there, I was angry, too. I went inside long enough to get my dress. I told him I'd bring the jeans back the next day, and left.

As soon as I got home, I put the dress in the back of the closet. I knew I couldn't be that young woman who had gazed back at me from the cloudy mirror the evening before. Nor could I fill the void that Jennifer had left.

WINDDRIFT

"In the cold air,
The spirit
Hardens."

THEODORE ROETHKE

onday evening I found a manila envelope from Eileen in my mailbox when I got home from the clinic.

I hadn't forgotten my conversation with her, but being with Jake these past few weeks, I'd stopped challenging him . . . and myself.

I went inside and put the envelope on my desk.

After dinner, I opened it.

"Dear Nora—

"Here's the bottom line about Luminex. You're dealing with a substance that has the potential to do grave harm, manufactured by a chemical company with political and economic clout. The regulatory agency responsible for taking on the chemical company is overworked, hypercautious, and easily intimidated (I'm being kind!).

"I've attached a list of the pesticides and herbicides manufactured by NUMAR Chemicals at their plants in the U.S., Mexico, and Honduras, and a toxicity profile on Luminex.

"I have a lot more to say, so I'll call you soon. Eileen."

I turned to the first sheet attached to her letter:

"NUMAR Chemical Company Products

"WEEDOUT—a defoliant and weedkiller sprayed on forests and rangelands; banned in 1983 for causing cancer and birth defects. NUMAR has asked for a reassessment based on their new research findings; status pending.

"FUMASOIL—a soil fumigant/insecticide; accidental spills have caused miscarriages in exposed women; currently being marketed and sold; targeted for a 'special review.'

"BUG-OUT—an insecticide; attacks the central nervous system in a manner similar to nerve gas; currently being marketed and sold; targeted for an 'accelerated review.'

"LUMINEX—a verdicide sprayed on forests and rangelands; suspected of causing cancer and birth defects; currently being marketed and sold."

She listed more chemical products, all similar, but I went on to the toxicity profile an independent laboratory had prepared. It explained how the verdicide altered the genetic behavior of plant cells. The report also said tests on animals strongly indicated that similar cell changes— breakages, or deletions of genetic material in egg and sperm cells—could occur in human beings and produce cancer or birth defects. Since even a single molecule of a gene-altering substance could affect genetic processes, the conclusion was that there could be no safe level of exposure.

I put the material back in the envelope and sat staring at it. Finally I put the envelope in my pocket, got in my Jeep, and drove to Jake's. His house was dark. When I walked up his porch steps and knocked on the door, I heard Magruder's soft whine.

After a few minutes, the porch light went on and Jake opened the door—looking sleepy, then pleased to see me. It was obvious he thought I'd come to make peace. "Nora . . . hi! Come in."

"Not tonight."

He took a closer look. "What's wrong?"

I held out the envelope. "Information about Luminex. And the company that makes it."

He flinched.

"Jake, you'd better read this."

"Where did you get it?"

"My friend, Eileen, in Washington."

For a moment he looked at me without speaking. Then: "I had hoped you'd given this up."

"Please take the envelope."

"Why? What do you expect me to do after I've read it?"

"Please! Just take a look."

He shook his head.

I left the envelope on his porch and went back down the steps.

"Nora!"

I didn't look back.

The next morning, he was waiting in his pick-up when I pulled into the clinic parking lot.

He came over as soon as I got out of the Jeep and handed me Eileen's envelope.

"Did you read what's inside?"

"No." He went on in a voice without emotion. "I can't be what you want me to be, and I can't do what you want me to do. I called my attorney. I'm activating the separation clause. He'll draw up the papers today."

I couldn't decipher the expression in his eyes, and it took me a couple of seconds to understand why. There wasn't any. He was looking at me as if I were a statue. When he'd threatened using the separation clause before, I'd told him I'd fight. Now I wasn't certain there was anyone to fight. I took a breath. "I guess that gives me sixty days."

"You can leave whenever you want. Tomorrow. Next week."

"I'm not going to do that."

He started toward his pick-up, then turned. "If you're planning some kind of campaign against the spraying, I want to know about it."

"I haven't decided yet what I'm going to do. When I know, I'll tell you."

He got into his truck and drove away.

STRESS WAS ONE THING I could blame for my missed menstrual

period. Also, tension. That had happened before.

But working with animals, you pick up the telltale signs: tender nipples and swollen breasts, increased appetite, an excessive need for sleep.

Jake and I hadn't used any birth control that first night.

I drove into Clarksville and picked up a pregnancy-testing kit, and on a Saturday afternoon four weeks after my missed period, did the test. Edgy and apprehensive when it was time to do the final litmus, I stood staring out the kitchen window. The garden hose lay in a coil, making me remember the day I'd been exposed to the spraying and how I'd felt trying to get Luminex off my body.

I completed the test, then watched the litmus take on color: positive. The next few moments, all I could think of was the toxicity profile Eileen had sent. It had explained how the toxic molecules had to bind to a receptor in the body before they could invade a sperm or egg cell's nucleus to get to its genetic material. But I hadn't been pregnant the morning of my exposure to Luminex. Maybe my body had leached all of it out.

That whole weekend my thoughts and emotions were on a roller coaster.

I couldn't deny the idea of a baby had an incredibly strong pull on me; maybe losing my parents at a young age made me want to parent my own child.

But what if something were wrong? The image of the calf I'd euthanized was vivid in my mind. And so was the anguish in Marilyn's eyes when she spoke of her mares' deformed foals.

I could probably use the toxicity profile on Luminex to make a good case for a legal therapeutic abortion, but . . . hour after hour, I seesawed back and forth, reaching no decision.

That week my temper grew as I coped with morning sickness, anxiety, fatigue, and mood swings. The night Eileen called wanting to talk about Luminex and the material she'd sent, I took her head off. Then I apologized, saying I was exhausted and that I'd call her back.

As Memorial Day weekend approached, I finally dialed her number. No answer. Saturday morning, I tried again. Still no answer. I was a little concerned, but the rest of the weekend was swept away by hard work. On Saturday, I ran a special clinic for young horse owners. At a fee they could afford, I filed their horses' teeth, gave tetanus and encephalitis shots, and took blood samples for the EIA test (making me remember that grim afternoon at the Dakin ranch with Jake).

From midnight to Sunday noon I was on call, and early Sunday morning Paul Milo telephoned. His deep voice was filled with tension as he said the milk from one of his Guernseys didn't look right.

When I pulled up in front of his ranch, he was waiting, and the sight of his pugnacious face cheered me more than anything had in days. As he led me out to his holding pen, he said he wished I'd told him that I was going to that town meeting because he'd have been there. "I had a stillborn calf this spring. I didn't call you because there wasn't a thing anybody could do."

"I'm sorry, Paul. I know you can't afford to lose any calves."

He nodded. "My best heifer's due to deliver soon. If something's wrong with *her* calf . . ." He shook his head.

"Was your ranch in the path of the spraying?"

"How the hell do I know? Depends on which way the wind was blowing." He looked at me. "I heard you got hit by some of that stuff."

I said irritably, "You must buy honey from Mavis Wilson," wondering crossly if she'd also managed to find out I was pregnant. Then I regretted my comment, realizing I was being foolish.

"She has the best honey around," Paul said equably. "And she doesn't mean any harm."

"I know," I sighed, and got busy taking supplies out of my kit.

Paul asked if I wanted any help.

"No, we'll be fine."

"Well, I'll be out by the barn if you need me."

I watched him walk away, almost wishing I'd asked him to stay, but talking about stillborn calves and Luminex made my stomach churn.

Speaking softly to calm the Guernsey, I took a milk sample from each of her teats, finding what I'd suspected. Normally, cows' milk is smooth, white, and creamy, but hers was full of white flakes. She had mastitis, a painful swelling of the milk glands usually caused when bacteria from the milking machines get inside an udder. It's common in dairy cows, but if the infection isn't treated quickly, it can spread to other parts of the cow's body and kill her. Fortunately Paul had called me at the first sign of distress. The shot of penicillin I gave her would most likely take care of it.

Rubbing protective salve on her teats, I found myself affected the way I often was these days when treating female animals—acutely sensitive of my pregnant body. The aureole around my nipples had deepened in color, and sometimes I just stood staring at my naked self in the cloudy bathroom mirror.

When I went to find Paul to tell him I'd be back to check on the Guernsey the middle of the next week, he was kneeling, mending a fence. He looked up at me. "You thinking about leaving Combsea?"

"Why?"

"Couple rumors."

God, I thought, does Mavis have a direct line to Jake's attorney? "There's a lot going on," I admitted.

He frowned. "I know people here feel pretty threatened. But maybe all they need is someone to show them how to stand up."

"Maybe." I started toward my Jeep.

"Nora?"

I turned.

"I hope you stay."

I smiled. "Thanks. I hope so, too."

I went to bed early that evening. I was doing that a lot lately.

When I arrived at the clinic Monday morning, Jake was in Winifred's office. He looked haggard, so I asked what was wrong.

Winifred answered for him. "He had to spend the night with a stud bull poisoned by veratrum. I'm rearranging his schedule so he can go home and rest."

Veratrum is a wild plant that blooms ferociously in the spring; its effects can be so toxic that twenty-four-hour observation of an affected animal is necessary. If things had been normal, Jake would have called me to relieve him.

"If there's anything I can do to help, let me know," I said.

Winifred nodded curtly.

I stood watching them for a minute, wanting to say something encouraging to Jake. But when he glanced up, his eyes were defensive, so I continued down the hall to my office.

Half an hour later, I was buried in the usual, heavy Monday morning workload, seeing sick or injured animals whose anxious owners had waited it out through the weekend. A little after ten, Winifred came to tell me I had a person-to-person long distance call.

I left the Irish setter I'd been working on with its owner and went into my office, thinking it might be Nell calling from London. A second later, I heard Eileen's voice.

"Nora?"

Her voice scared me it was so thin—as if its texture had been separated into strands, and only one was still connected. "I've been trying to reach you," I said. "What's going on?"

"The doctors call it an 'exacerbation.' I call it fighting dirty. MS is good at that."

For a moment, I couldn't speak. "How bad?"

"Bad. For a while, I was blind."

"When did it happen?"

"About ten days ago."

"Why didn't you call me?"

"Until now, I couldn't call anybody."

"Where are you?"

"In Boston."

"With your parents?"

"No. I'm still in the hospital. Been here a week. They're about ready to kick me out."

"Are you going to your parents' house?"

"Not by choice." She gave a thready little laugh.

"Do you want me to come there?"

"No. I was wondering if I could come to Combsea."

I was so surprised, it took me a minute.

"I guess that's a terrible idea."

"No," I said quickly. "It's okay, it's fine. When do you want to come?"

"Tomorrow. Wait. Hey, it doesn't have to be tomorrow."

"Tomorrow's fine."

"Then can you meet me at the San Francisco Airport? There's a flight that gets in at 5 p.m."

"Sure," I said, my mind racing ahead to figure out whether I really could.

"Nora? I'll be in a wheelchair. Don't be shocked."

"You were in a wheelchair the day we met, remember?"

"Yeah."

We hung up.

I hurried down the hallway to Winifred's office to tell her about Eileen and that I had to drive to San Francisco in the morning. "Can you and Jake handle things?"

"We managed for quite a few years. I gather we soon will be again."

I left before saying something I'd regret, went back to my office, finished removing fox burrs from the Irish setter's ears, and when I was alone, scanned my appointments for the next day. Noticing I was scheduled to go to the O'Hare ranch to check a cranky broodmare, I telephoned Marilyn to ask if I could stop by late that afternoon instead, and she said, "Sure."

Then I called Jake. I could tell from his voice that I had awakened him.

"What's going on? Is there an emergency?"

"Yes," I said, "a personal one." And I told him about Eileen.

"Is R&R the only reason your friend is coming to Combsea?"

"What's that supposed to mean?"

"She's the one who sent you the information about Luminex, right?"

Suddenly the whole damned week crashed down on me. I said, "I'm coming over there. Right now."

Five minutes later, I was at his door.

He still hadn't shaved. There were deep circles under his eyes. He looked like hell. I didn't care.

"I'd rather tell you this inside. But I'll do it standing here on the porch if I have to."

He moved away from the door.

I went into the living room and faced him. "I'm pregnant."

"You're—" his voice constricted. The hard expression softened, and his face looked more alive than it had in days. He started toward me, but I put my hand up and he stayed where he was.

"I hadn't planned on telling you because I don't know what's going to happen to this baby—whether I can carry it to term, or should even try after being exposed to the spraying. Until I get control of my emotions, I don't know what I'm going to do. Which brings me to your question. My friend is coming here to recover from an illness. If she gets better and we decide to take on Luminex, you'll be the first to know."

I started for the door.

"Nora?"

I turned.

His expression was tormented. "If you have the baby—"

I didn't let him finish. "If that happens, we'll talk about it."

I DROVE OUT TO MARILYN'S late that afternoon, making her ranch my last appointment of the day. The source of her mare's irritability was an infected tooth. I wished my problems could be as easily solved.

Marilyn invited me in afterward for a cup of coffee. As I was spooning sugar into my cup, I spilled it all over the table. "Shit! I can't do anything right today."

While she helped me clean up the mess she asked what was going on. I told her about Eileen.

After I'd finished, she wanted to know, "How are you going to manage?"

I didn't have a ready answer. In the interim since Eileen's call, I'd already realized my house was primitive and isolated and my workday long. I wasn't certain yet how we'd manage, only that we would.

Marilyn said, "Mel's niece is graduating from high school next week and is already looking for a job. She's helped out around here a few times and seems pretty sensible. I bet she'd be happy to go out to your place and stay with Eileen. She could use Mel's car or my pick-up to drive her anywhere she wants to go."

Grateful for her practicality and even less able than usual to respond to kindness with equanimity, I blinked away sudden tears. "That would help a lot. Thanks."

Marilyn reached across the table and put her hand on my arm. "Women in the first trimester are usually over-emotional."

I stared at her, then asked, "How did you find out I'm pregnant? I haven't said anything to anyone—until today."

"I raise broodmares, remember? And I care about you, so I pay attention. It's in the skin, the eyes." She smiled. "And especially the temper." She paused. "I assume Jake's the father?"

I nodded ruefully. "Yeah. I lost my temper before I came out here today and I told him about the baby. Now I wish I hadn't said anything."

"Why?"

"I'm too worried."

In a split second, her face told me she knew what I meant, and such swift understanding reinforced my anxiety. Then she said, "It was right to tell him. Why protect him?"

"Things are awful between us."

"All the more reason. Have you seen a doctor?"

"Not yet. I'm going to."

"I know a good obstetrician in Clarksville. Her name is Dr. Kester."

I said I'd make an appointment as soon as I had Eileen settled.

Walking me out to the Jeep, Marilyn put a reassuring arm around my shoulders. "You're going to do fine. Like Purity."

I wanted to believe her.

ON THE WAY HOME, I shopped, picking out some items at the market I knew Eileen liked, and getting a couple of boards at the hardware store. When I got to the cabin, I put the boards over my steps so Eileen could propel her wheelchair over them. Then I puttered around my house, emptying my things out of the bottom two drawers of the bureau in the alcove where she would sleep. I'd take the living room sofa. Other than that, there just wasn't a lot to do. Since the place was so sparsely furnished, little would impede her wheelchair. The low brick-and-board bookcases I'd put up would give her easy access to my "library." If she could negotiate the front yard, I'd clear a path to the edge of the pine grove.

Too keyed up to sleep much, I was on the road by five the next morning. I'd decided to take the forty-mile cut over to the coast and drive south on Highway 101 at least as far as Arcata, so I could see the place where the Combsea River met the ocean. When the trees bordering the highway changed to groves of beach pine and Sitka spruce, I knew I was nearing the coast. Before I could see the ocean, I could smell the salt spray and hear the waves. Then suddenly, there it was with the river flowing into it. I'd never seen a seascape like it. The mouth of the river created a palette of sand, and the wind and waves played with it, forming small dunes, and behind the dunes, hollows filled with golden grasses. I parked and got out of the jeep, climbed to the top of one of the dunes, and watched the river flowing into the ocean and two herons flying low above the water. One of them dropped to a hollow behind the dunes and stalked through the grass on stilt-like legs, using its long neck like a periscope as it searched for food. The other one flew on alone. Suddenly I was so filled with thoughts of Timothy, I sank down on the sand and sat rocking back and forth watching the solitary heron. Afterward, I knew there was one more place I had to visit.

Near Arcata, the highway curved away from the coast to meander in and out of the Humboldt Redwoods. Deep within one of the groves, I pulled off the road and got out. Kneeling to touch the tree roots, I saw the life they nurtured: mosses and ferns and pale, delicate wild flowers. Sunshine penetrating the mist and sea fog descended through the canopy of branches, and I could hear a warbler's voice blending with a nearby stream's rush. Every now and then, tree branches moving in the wind made a sound like breathing. For the first time since his death, my thoughts of Timothy were peaceful.

I was determined that Eileen should see these trees. If we spent the night in Sausalito and were on the road by seven, we might be able to reach the redwoods by noon. Depending, of course, on how well Eileen could tolerate long hours of driving.

Below Eureka, the highway widened into four lanes. As the traffic grew heavier, my mind dipped into memories of the Berkeley years with Eileen and the times I'd been afraid for her after she'd pushed herself to the limit. How ironic that she should have had an exacerbation now, when the firm she worked for tried so hard to safeguard her. Reflecting on this history made me consider for the first time that perhaps she did need to push herself hard; maybe that's what kept her going.

It was mid-afternoon when I arrived in Sausalito, where I booked a room for us at a waterfront hotel.

A little after five, I was inside the airport terminal.

Emerging from the jetway, Eileen was operating her own wheel-chair, but an airline employee assigned to accompany the handicapped walked beside her.

I wasn't prepared for the change. My immediate impression was that her eyes had gotten bigger. But that wasn't it. She'd lost so much weight, her eyes looked much too large for her face. I also thought the blouse she wore—with its long, full sleeves—was intended to conceal how thin her arms were.

But her smile melted my fear, and seconds later I was on my knees, awkwardly hugging her. When I drew back, some of the tears streaking my face were hers. She opened her purse, took out two tissues, and handed me one. We wiped, blew, and laughed until Eileen said, "Could we get out of here? We're making a spectacle."

Walking beside her down the long corridor to the baggage terminal, I observed she'd lost none of her skill in negotiating her wheelchair through crowds. While we waited to collect her luggage, she stared combatively at adults who gaped when her legs jerked with spasms, but smiled reassuringly at a couple of children who also stared.

She only had two suitcases, and I'd found a parking place close to the terminal exit. Within minutes, we were on the freeway. Driving through the heavy rush-hour traffic, we didn't talk much. But crossing Golden Gate Bridge, she exclaimed softly over remembered land-marks. Entering the long Marin County tunnel, she was silent again until we came out into the light. Then, giving me a quick sidelong glance, she said, "I'm beginning to wonder if I should believe every-thing you've been telling me about Combsea. You have a glow, Nora."

For days, I'd tried—unsuccessfully—to think of ways to tell Eileen. Now she was here, and I simply came out with it. "I'm pregnant."

"My god . . ." She tried to collect herself and ended up joking. "Well, let's see. It's not your landlord; he's eighty-something. That leaves the owner of the feed and tack store and that dairy farmer—"

"Jake."

I didn't say anything more. I felt her eyes on my face, but she didn't press it, asking simply, "How long have you known?"

"A few weeks."

"Why didn't you tell me?"

Seeing a turn-out ahead, I parked there and told her about the day of the spraying, minimizing it as much as possible. However, like me, she knew too much.

"Oh, damn," she whispered, "damn, damn." She rested her head on the passenger window and closed her eyes. Abruptly I was ashamed. She'd come to me to recover, yet here I was piling more rocks on her shoulders, needing to rely on her courage and resilience.

IT WAS A LITTLE PAST EIGHT when we went downstairs to the hotel's small dining room. We were both too tired to eat much but sat watching fishing trawlers on the bay. Finally we left half our food and went back to the room.

It could have been moonlight streaming through the window that woke me a few hours later, or the unfamiliar sound of waves lapping the hotel docks, but I believe some part of me knew Eileen wasn't sleeping.

I glanced over.

She lay with her face turned toward the window, her profile illuminated by the silvery gray light.

"Hey?"

She turned.

"You okay?"

"Well, I'd better be since I'm going to be an aunt." Her voice sounded stronger than it had that afternoon.

"Aunt and godmother," I said. "What were you thinking about?"

She gave an impatient little shake of her head. "Things that begin with 'M'—maternity, mother's milk, muumuus . . ." And with the old sly toughness, "Mayhem." Then: "Is your pregnancy the reason you wouldn't discuss the material I sent you about Luminex?"

"Yes."

"Does all this mean you want me to take off my thinking cap?"

I was honest. "I don't know." And then I added, "For your own sake, I think you should put it on hold."

"Shit, you sound like the partners at the firm," she said, adding after a moment, "I decide what's best for my sake."

MORNING SUN SHINING DIRECTLY in our faces woke us up before eight. I watched Eileen move her legs toward the edge of the bed, and that was as far as she got. I remembered how, when she was overtired at Berkeley, she could move only slowly during the first half hour after waking. I massaged her legs and helped her into the shower, knowing we were never going to make the redwoods by noon, but holding onto the hope that if we got a move on, we could be there before dark.

I showered and dressed while she put on her makeup and combed her hair, meticulous as always. Once, in the Benvenue house when I'd been trying to get her to hurry, she'd snapped, "Look. It's perfectly okay for you to go out with your hair in tangles. If I do that, people stare at me and think, 'Oh, the poor thing.' If I can avoid pity by spending two hours getting ready to face the world, I'll do it."

It was midmorning by the time we left the hotel.

Making up for our meager appetites the night before, we stopped at a roadside café and put away breakfasts that would have done a trucker proud. I hoped they'd last us for two hundred fifty miles because I didn't want to stop until the redwoods. More than ever, I wanted Eileen to see the trees.

She dozed on and off while I drove north as fast as the law allowed. We reached Leggett by late afternoon and, after a quick supper, continued north, entering the redwoods at twilight as I'd hoped. Everything I'd seen the previous day was touched with mystery just before nightfall. The smoky green light was darker, denser. And the birds' voices brought the air to life, making me remember something Timothy had written after he'd spent the night here: "Now I know how the old stories of enchanted forests began."

After we'd gone a few miles, Eileen asked, "Could we stop?" I pulled over, and we sat watching the deepening light. She said, "Could we get out?"

The soft carpet of needles and moss accepted her chair, and as I walked beside her, I could tell she was seeing everything: the ferns, the wildflowers. She stopped once to bend over and touch some tiny phantom orchids, and the expression on her face matched the feeling I'd had when I'd stood listening to the branches breathing the day before.

We stayed outside until it was almost dark and the sea fog swept in; then we couldn't see, but we could hear the soft dripping of the water slipping off the branches.

Eileen asked, "Could we stay here, Nora, until the sun comes up?"

I had enough blankets in the Jeep to arrange makeshift beds, one across the rear seat and one in the back. Soon we were settled, our heads propped up on blanketroll pillows. Neither of us felt sleepy; we wanted to talk and relish the forest and each other's company. I spoke about Marilyn and Purity and Crusoe—not at all about Jake—and Eileen told me she'd run into Rupert and they were seeing each other quite often. He'd taken Florynce Kennedy's advice and was trying to "kick butt on Wall Street." But his trials frequently brought him to Washington, and he'd recently suggested he and Eileen co-buy a townhouse.

"But that was before I got sicker."

The conversation faded. After a while, we slept.

It was probably around four o'clock in the morning when she woke me, whispering softly, "Nora, I have to pee."

I didn't bother with the wheelchair, just sort of slid her horizontally out of the Jeep, then held her under her arms. The fog touched us like satin rain.

Pulling down her jeans, Eileen whispered, "I'll never forget this moment. What a . . . a spiritual pee." We both started laughing.

After this excursion, our clothes were clammy from the fog. Inside the Jeep, I lit the Coleman lantern and got dry things out of our suitcases. As we were changing, Eileen looked shyly at my belly that didn't yet show my pregnancy and asked if she could put her hands there. I nodded. The touch of her fingers was like someone casting a friendly spell.

An hour later, we were watching the great trees greet the sunrise.

EILEEN EXPLORED MY HOUSE like a ground hog inspecting a burrow. She wheeled up to the kitchen table to test its height for reading and eating, then went around the living room, pausing to scan book titles on my shelves. Observing my cluttered desk, she murmured, "That's what *my* desk looks like." Then she moved on into the sleeping alcove, felt the mattress, nodded, and said, "This is a good hotel. I think I'll stay."

"You missed the best part."

"What?"

"Look out the windows."

She went from window to window, lingering at the one above my desk that faced the pine grove. She nodded. "It'll do."

After we'd unpacked her suitcases, we sat on the porch swing watching the stars grow brighter as night fell on Combsea.

Rupert called the next day and gave her bloody hell for sneaking out on him. She said, "I didn't sneak, I left . . . what did you want me to do, invite you to come along?"

I smiled at hearing the old feistiness in her voice. But I also noticed how distracted she looked when she put down the phone.

"Are you going to keep seeing him?"

She sighed. "I don't know."

By the end of the first week, we'd established a routine. I'd cook breakfast, and while I was getting ready for work, Eileen did the dishes. Mel's niece, Beth, a plump, cheerful eighteen-year-old, rode her bicycle to the house every morning and stayed until mid-afternoon. A quick learner, she was soon able to help with Eileen's physical therapy, so between that and a good diet, Eileen started gaining weight, getting color back, and improving her fine motor control.

However, a few days later when Marilyn invited us both to dinner, Eileen said she'd prefer to postpone seeing the O'Hare ranch and even meeting Marilyn until she was stronger. I sensed other reasons behind her hesitation. We hadn't discussed Luminex since that night in the hotel room. The subject was in limbo.

My feelings were in a snarl. I was still unwilling to let thoughts about Luminex co-exist with my pregnancy. And I was worried that Eileen's getting more deeply involved would affect her recovery.

AT THE END OF EILEEN'S third week in Combsea, I came home from the clinic to find her getting around the house on her walking sticks.

After dinner that night, I started mending a pair of jeans while Eileen did some hand-clench exercises with a rubber ball. She was quieter than usual, but, sensing what was on her mind, it didn't surprise me when she said, "Beth has the use of Mel's car tomorrow. She offered to drive me out to Marilyn's ranch."

"Oh? Have you called Marilyn?"

"Not yet. I wanted to see how you felt about it."

"I think it would do you good. Really. It's time you two met."

Pricking my forefinger with the needle point, I swore softly and put down the jeans. "Look, just go ahead and talk to her about the moratorium and Luminex. Do whatever you have to. Just leave me out of it! Okay?"

"Sure. If that's what you want."

The next day, I kept thinking about Eileen's visit to the O'Hare ranch and what might come out of it.

But when I got home, she talked only about how beautiful the ranch and the horses were—especially Purity.

On Saturday, however, she asked me to drive her into Clarksville to buy a laptop computer. Learning from the clerk that it would take a week to get one shipped from Sacramento, she wrote the check for the purchase with sharp, irritable strokes and muttered darkly about living in the boondocks as we were leaving the store. Obviously something was going on, but she was doing exactly as I'd asked: leaving me out of it.

A few evenings later, I found her seated at the kitchen table going through a shoebox filled with file cards. She was so absorbed she said, "Hi," without even looking up.

"What have you got there?"

A little shrug. "Just some stuff Marilyn gave me." She put the lid on the shoebox. "Whose turn is it to cook?"

The day her laptop arrived, she asked if she could have the toxicity profile on Luminex she'd sent me so she could share it with Marilyn. I had to fight a stab of envy before I could say, "Sure, it's in the top drawer of my desk."

From then on, the steady tapping of her fingertips on the computer keyboard followed me out to the jeep most mornings as I left for work and greeted me when I got home. I'd never been so at odds with myself. Even though I knew I wasn't being excluded—that I was excluding myself—I felt resentful as hell.

AS THE LONG FOURTH OF JULY weekend approached, I looked forward to a few days' respite from the clinic. Whenever Jake and I had to work together, or even be in the supply room at the same time, it was an ordeal. If even our elbows brushed, we moved quickly away from each other.

The day preceding a holiday weekend is usually hectic, and that Thursday was no exception. Just as I was leaving on afternoon rounds, Winifred ran out to the parking lot to tell me Paul Milo had called. His prize heifer had calved the day before, and when he went out to check on her, he'd found her down. He was pretty sure it was milk fever.

Sometimes, after giving birth, a cow will use up most of her own calcium to make milk for her calf. Then her muscles get so weak she collapses and can't move. If she isn't given more calcium quickly, she'll die.

I drove to Paul's ranch as fast as I could. I found him in the birthing pasture down on his knees beside the animal, holding her head in his lap, stroking her and talking softly, all his strength channeled into comforting.

I knelt beside him. The cow's head was twisted sideways, her eyes were dull, her nose dry, her legs cool to the touch—all classic signs of milk fever.

The calf was standing alone in a nearby grove of trees. Every time it cried, the heifer tried to lift her head.

Paul said grimly, "I can't lose this heifer."

"You won't."

I inserted a small rubber hose into a calcium bottle and gave Paul the bottle to hold.

"What's her name?"

"Miranda."

I knelt and put a catheter in the jugular vein in Miranda's neck and inserted the rubber hose into the catheter. For the next ten minutes, Paul held the bottle while I monitored the flow. Too much calcium rushing through her heart could cause it to stop beating.

Calcium works fast. By the time the bottle was empty, she was looking a lot better, but we were going to have to force her to get up in order to get her circulation moving. Cows get up hind legs first. I'd often wondered how they were able to, when their bodies are so heavy and their legs seem so fragile. Paul went to the barn to get a prod, and I spoke softly to Miranda telling her firmly exactly what she was going to have to do. Moments later, Paul was giving her mild shocks with the prod, and I was yelling encouragement like a high school cheerleader. I felt foolish, but I'd done it before with animals who were down and it seemed to help.

Miranda moved her head slowly from side to side, got her hind legs up, and gazed at me out of her great cow eyes. "Yea, Miranda!" I shouted, "You can do it!"

Finally, she was up on all four legs.

Paul and I grinned at each other. In a few hours, Miranda would be well enough to be with her calf.

"Bull or heifer?" I asked as we were walking back to my jeep.

"Heifer. Named her Lucy. You remember the song . . . 'Lucy in the Sky with Diamonds'?"

"Yeah," I said softly. "I remember."

"Thanks for coming so fast."

"It's my job."

"You yelled good. Maybe you could use a cheering section yourself, Nora. I'm available."

"That would make an army of two," I murmured.

"And you'd want to be the general, right?"

Then he surprised me by touching the tip of my nose with his forefinger. "Speck of dust," he explained. His hands were large and calloused. I stared at them, and then at him.

His smile was slow. "Like I keep telling you . . . I'm here."

I HAD TROUBLE GETTING to sleep that night—which often happened lately. Finally I drifted off, thinking of Paul.

However, a couple of hours later a sharp pain woke me. Then I felt the bleeding. Moaning softly, I lay still, not even wanting to breathe, only to stop this wicked flow.

I heard Eileen stir.

"Nora?"

I didn't answer.

More urgently: "Nora?"

"I'm bleeding."

"Oh, god."

"I don't think I should move; do you?"

"No. Lie still!"

I heard her get out of bed, the soft thudding of her walking sticks, and then she was next to me, her hand finding mine. She said, "Do you want me to call a doctor?"

"I haven't been to a doctor. I was going to go to one Marilyn told me about."

"I'll call Marilyn."

The phone was on a low table near the sofa. She turned on the lamp next to it. We blinked and stared at each other in the sudden brightness.

Then she picked up the phone and dialed Marilyn. "It's Eileen. Nora's bleeding." A moment later, she replaced the receiver, came back to me and took my hand again. "She's coming. And she's calling Dr. Kester."

I lay still, my eyes closed. The pain—a dull twisting inside me—was heightened by my terror, helplessness, and grief. I was losing this baby.

I have no idea how long it was before I heard Eileen open the door, then Marilyn's voice, and a few minutes later, another voice. Footsteps on the pine floor. "Nora?"

I opened my eyes.

"I'm Dr. Kester. I'm going to examine you."

"Okay."

A few minutes later, she told me she could admit me to the hospital if I wanted to go there, or she could take care of me here.

I said I wanted to stay in my house.

Dr. Kester was gentle, efficient, and comforting, but the next hour was a blur of pain and anger.

When it was over, she told me to come to her office on Monday for an examination. Then she touched my arm and said, "The emotional damage from these things is always worse than the physical, so give yourself a lot of room, Nora. You'll need it."

When she and Marilyn left, Eileen went with them to the porch. Through the open door, I could see sunrise coloring tree branches, lining pine needles with light. Suddenly my sense of loss became unbearable. Sobs began to come from a place in me I hadn't known existed, gathering strength to force their way out, like prisoners pulling down a jail. They pushed on and on until the last one had escaped. Only then did they let me go, and sleep blanketed my mind.

THE NEXT DAY, Eileen insisted I rest on the bed in the alcove and I didn't argue. Tears would ebb, then flow. I'd sleep, then wake. All day, all night. I was in some other world.

I was aware of Eileen pacing on her walking sticks, staring out the window, asking softly if I needed anything, encouraging me to eat or drink something.

On Sunday morning, Marilyn came back. She was carrying several boxes like the ones I'd seen Eileen poring through. She put them on the kitchen table, then sat on the edge of my bed. Taking my hand, she said, "Nothing I can say is going to make what's happened easier. But it is important for you to know you're not alone. I want you to read the files Eileen and I have been working on."

"Maybe tomorrow."

Eileen moved to stand beside Marilyn. "Now would be better."

I wanted to yell at them both to leave me alone, but biting down on my anger, I withdrew my hand from Marilyn's, got out of bed, and went into the bathroom. I had an overwhelming urge to lock the door, sit on the floor, and stay there.

I undressed slowly, stepped into the shower, turned on the spigots, and stood under the hot water, soaping myself—almost angrily at first; then, crying, I washed my body as though I were granting it absolution. Finally, I turned off the water and reached for a towel. Pulling my damp hair back into its barrette and putting on some clothes, I began to feel more familiar to myself. Yet I knew something in me had changed that would not change back.

Marilyn and Eileen were seated at the kitchen table when I came out. Eileen's eyes met mine.

"Okay," I said.

I sat down, and Marilyn took the lid off one of the boxes and pushed it toward me.

I lifted out a thick packet labeled, "Three Rivers, Oregon." As I removed the rubber band, Eileen said, "That packet is from one of the heaviest spraying areas. Read some of the cards out loud, Nora, please."

For the next several minutes, I read accounts written by mothers whose young children had had severe pneumonia-like illnesses. Others written by animal owners whose cats, dogs, horses, and cows developed tumors all over their bodies, causing such pain that the owners had them put to death or shot them. More by naturalists who had observed whole flocks of birds with eyes swollen shut, unable to fly; songbird nests empty except for those holding corpses; fish floating dead in the rivers or beached on the shore, and otters used to feeding on them dead of starvation.

My throat began to ache and I closed my eyes.

Eileen took the packet and said, "That's enough for now."

I CONTINUED READING THE MATERIAL in Marilyn's boxes that afternoon while Eileen worked steadily at her laptop. Before, I'd suspected how hard she was working. Watching her now, I longed to be part of it.

Sunday night I told her I was ready to rejoin the fight and asked her to explain exactly what she'd been up to.

She sat down tiredly on the sofa and put her feet up. "Okay. After I found out the extent of Marilyn's networking, I called the firm. They've agreed to my exploring possible legal action against the makers of Luminex if I can get support from people who've been affected by it." She seemed lost in thought for a minute. "Assuming I get that support, I still have to figure out the best road to take so I can present a definite plan for the firm's approval. I do know one thing."

"What?"

"I'm not going for a class action suit. I learned in the Guatemalan case that corporate attorneys for chemical companies are masters at keeping such cases out of the court system for years. And as the months of pretrial depositions and hearings go on and people's health deteriorates because of whatever they were exposed to, they get doubtful, impatient, frustrated—to say nothing of poor. Eventually a lot of them become willing to accept out-of-court settlement offers rather than go through long, unpredictable trials.

"That's the first stumbling block. Next is the issue of how to place blame. The outcome of class action suits involving hazardous substances always hangs on the words, 'but for.' Would people claiming damage have escaped damage 'but for' exposure to the chemical. A woman exposed to Luminex spraying in Three Rivers, Oregon, is dying of cancer right now. If she were involved in a class action suit, the jury would have to answer the question: would she have escaped cancer 'but for' her exposure to Luminex?"

"Well, of course she would," I said.

"Could you prove that?" Eileen asked. "How would you go about convincing a judge and jury that out of all the contaminants that the woman was exposed to in her lifetime, one particular substance actually caused her cancer? Like you, Nora. You might have had a spontaneous abortion regardless of your exposure to Luminex. You've been under stress; you encounter strong chemicals in your work; you may even be genetically predisposed to aborting. A good corporate attorney would use all those things against you."

"Are you telling me Luminex is innocent until proven guilty, just like an accused murderer?"

"Actually, far greater proof is required against a chemical than a person. Death or injury caused by an individual can usually be attributed to that individual's actions. But the same things that affect people who have been exposed to chemical substances—cancer, miscarriages, children born with defects—strike others who have never been near those substances."

"For god's sake!" I exploded. "Even if we find people in Combsea willing to file a class action suit, you're saying they wouldn't stand a chance?"

"I can't say for certain. I'm simply pointing out the risks. And here's another one. Even with a strong case and staunch people, you can still lose, because so much depends on the political climate."

"How?" I asked.

"Well, let's go back to the fifties, when the government expanded the testing of nuclear weapons. The Nevada nuclear test site was forty miles away from where a group of Utah sheep ranchers wintered their sheep. In the spring of 1953, those ranchers lost more than forty-five hundred head. On the verge of bankruptcy, they united to bring a class action suit against the government, charging their sheep's deaths were due to exposure to radiation. They hung together, refused settlement offers, and their case was brilliantly presented. But the court's ruling went against them because the ranchers were opposing the power of a government determined to build its nuclear arsenal."

"And today?"

"Today, high-tech chemistry or weaponry—high-tech anything—has clout."

"Has a class action suit against a chemical company ever succeeded?"

"A few times . . . when the evidence was undeniable. It happened, for example, with Thalidomide. I guess some people might say the Vietnam veterans won against Agent Orange. But to me, that was a murky victory."

I couldn't find a chink of light in the picture she'd painted. Yet the expression in her eyes was summoning a memory of the optimism I'd seen when she was fighting for people's rights in Berkeley. "Is there another option?"

"I'm working on it." She paused. "You probably know by now, Nora, my motives aren't unselfish. This battle between people and toxic chemicals is the first stage of a law-science confrontation that's going to last for decades. If I can be on the barricades for that, my life will have made some kind of sense."

That was the first time I totally understood that her commitment was connected to something so elemental it would survive no matter what MS inflicted on her. The reason I understood was because I felt the same force stirring in me.

I grinned at Eileen.

Then I whispered, "Are you ready, Luminex? Can you hear us coming?"

ON MONDAY MORNING, I drove into Clarksville to see Dr. Kester.

The nurse ushered me into an examining room, instructed me to take off my clothes and slip into a paper hospital gown, then sit on the examining table. Dr. Kester appeared a few moments later. I remembered her gentleness—but I don't think I'd even been aware of what she looked like. She had short gray hair and a face that might have been stern except for the laugh lines around her mouth. Behind her glasses, her eyes were kind.

She took my hand and held it for a moment and asked how I was.

"Better," I said.

"Good. Let's have a look."

After examining me and pronouncing, "Everything's fine," she asked if I planned on getting pregnant again soon.

I hadn't expected the question, and my swift, strong response, "Not until things change," startled me until I realized it was tapping into all the fury I'd kept locked up while carrying Jake's and my child.

Dr. Kester looked at me intently. "Do you mean, not until you're one hundred percent positive you can give birth to a normal child?"

"Not only me," I said.

"Marilyn told me about your exposure to Luminex," she said quietly. "But Nora, no woman has any guarantees in childbirth. A fifth of all pregnancies end spontaneously in the first month before women even know they're pregnant, and another ten percent result in miscarriages after the pregnancy becomes apparent."

"Why is that?" I demanded.

"Partly because we live in a world in which scientists synthesize millions of new chemicals every year and people swallow drugs by the gross and are exposed to waste and pollutants we haven't even identified yet."

Again, the plumb line tapped into rage. "Then it's time the people who load the dice stop being allowed to walk away from the table."

"You're talking about chemical manufacturers?"

"For starters."

"They live in steel houses, Nora."

"Maybe. But that's not going to stop us."

" 'Us'?"

"Marilyn and Eileen and me."

"What do you plan to do?"

"Right now we're exploring our options."

Then I asked if she'd been aware of an increase in miscarriages among her patients in the years since the Luminex spraying had begun.

Frowning, she said she thought perhaps there had been but she hadn't done an actual case count.

"Would you be willing to do one?"

"I don't see why not."

"Could you also tell me if miscarriages increased sharply in the spring months following a spraying?"

She nodded. "Call me in a couple of weeks."

"I will." I put on my jacket and turned to leave. As I opened the door, she said, "If the numbers turn out to be significant, what are you going to do with that information?"

"Use it."

I CALLED JAKE THAT EVENING and asked if I could speak to him in his office the next morning before he left on his rounds.

Eileen was watching and listening.

He asked, "Does this have something to do with the clinic?"

"No."

He hesitated. "Six-thirty too early for you?"

"I'll be there."

After I hung up, Eileen said, "I've never met the man. Yet I almost feel I know him." She paused. "Marilyn seems fond of him."

"So am I. But he won't let old wounds heal. His life is just being swallowed up." I looked at Eileen. "Like mine almost was."

Lying in bed that night, I listened to a pair of pygmy owls calling back and forth, singing the same note over and over. They sounded like lost children. In my dreams, that's what they became.

Jake's pick-up was all by itself in the parking lot when I pulled up beside it, and I was relieved this wasn't one of Winifred's early mornings.

His office was dark, but the light was on in the supply room. He was filling up his kit bag. He stopped when he saw me. I'd never noticed the way the fluorescent light accentuated the deep lines in his face. But I couldn't think about his sadness now. I said, "I lost the baby, Jake."

As he closed the cupboard and turned away, the vulnerable slump of his shoulders that used to make me want to comfort him suddenly had the opposite effect. "Go ahead," I said, "turn your back! I *know* my being exposed to Luminex killed our baby. And now more than ever, I have to fight. But not you, right? You're going to keep your life in a cotton-lined box. But it doesn't protect you from pain, does it? The only thing it protects you from is change. And some day you're going to find out everything's changed but you. And then you'll know you've made your own hell. Because that's the only place where nothing ever changes."

He turned and looked at me with tormented eyes. "If you hadn't come here, things would have stayed the same."

"No, they wouldn't. They would have gotten worse. More deformed animals, more women having miscarriages. *Somebody* would have said, 'That's enough.'"

"It wouldn't have been me. I'm not a fighter. I never have been, and I never will be." Then his eyes held mine. "But I want you to know how deeply sorry I am you lost the baby."

"Not 'the' baby," I said. "*Our* baby."

He flinched and walked past me out of the room.

A moment later, I heard his truck door open and shut. Then silence.

I went into his office and looked out the window. He was sitting behind the wheel. His head was down. I think he was crying.

Yet I knew now, the only kind of love he would accept could demand nothing from him, threaten him in no way. It had to be static, change-less, totally accepting of his passivity.

I turned away from the window and went down the hall to my own office.

A few minutes later, I heard him drive away.

WHILE EILEEN WAS WASHING the dinner dishes that night, I went outside for a short walk. I watched a swallow darting among the bushes, then stood listening as a ground squirrel gave the long, whistling alarm call signaling a predator was near.

"Nora?"

I turned. Eileen was standing in the doorway.

"Hm?"

"Feel like talking?"

"Sure."

I followed her back inside, leaving the door open. The sound of soft-winged insects batting against the screen was the only sound in the room until she said, "I've decided on the road I want us to take.

You remember reading, in the toxicity report I sent you, how damning the animal test results were on Luminex?"

"Yes."

She stood up and started pacing the room on her walking sticks.

"If a chemical is suspected to be acutely toxic to people exposed to it over a period of time, and those people put together a case tallying its risks, an administrative law court can order the manufacturer to present a case showing how that product benefits society. Then it will be up to a judge to decide whether the benefits outweigh the risks or vice versa, and whether or not the chemical's registration should be revoked.

"But here's the key: administrative law hearings require judges to take animal tests into consideration; whereas in civil courts, those test results can be ignored. Or worse, ridiculed by chemical company lawyers."

"Where and how do we begin?"

She smiled. "That's a terrific word."

"What?"

" 'We.' " Then she went on briskly, "All the material Marilyn has gathered in her networking is useful because it built, in me, a conviction about what's happening that I can communicate in court. In fact, I used a lot of her material to convince the firm to let me take this on. But, geographically, her data is too widespread, and, chronologically, it's too vague. I need concentrated areas with verifiable spraying dates matching specific outcomes. You're going to have to get people to sign written statements and submit themselves and/or their animals for examination.

"It'll mean risk for you—and them. People who come out against Luminex could be exposed to harassment of various kinds; some could lose their jobs. Marilyn's behind on paying her bills, so if the utility companies decide to cut her off, they can. God knows what else will happen. And it's going to be completely up to you because I can't even be on the battlefront here. Next week, I have to fly back to Washington, start conferring with the other lawyers at the firm, and put in a lot of time getting the groundwork set up.

"But remember this: Every scrap of evidence you turn up is going to be important. Whether or not it finds its way into my brief or a discussion of the issues, it'll find its way into my brain, and it will be used."

I couldn't sleep that night. I tossed and turned on the sofa until my bones revolted. Trying to be quiet and not wake Eileen, I got up and went to my desk. I took out the package from Ken that had been buried unopened in my drawer for so long and removed the wrapping. The label on the box said, "Ancestral grasses/Kuwait." I lifted the lid. Seeds . . . there were probably two dozen seeds inside. I picked up one and held it in the palm of my hand, remembering the story of the Barberry ants. If seeds from Asia could grow in the Pacific Northwest, Timothy knew these seeds from Kuwait could grow in California.

The next day, Eileen helped me plant them in the pine grove.

EILEEN SPENT THE NEXT forty-eight hours organizing her papers and packing them in two huge suitcases she borrowed from Marilyn.

The day before she was to leave, Rupert called. I was in the kitchen and heard her "Mmm-hmm's," and "uh-huh's," and wondered what was going on. After she hung up, she told me. "He's found a town-house he wants me to look at."

"Are you going to?"

"I don't know. The stages of this damn disease are seared across my mind: benign, exacerbating-remitting, chronic-relapsing, chronic-progressive. I'm in remission now, but for how long? God, I don't want him pitying me." She shook her head. "Well, we'll see."

She'd made arrangements with Beth to drive her to the airport the next day. We went to bed early and got up at dawn. Beth pulled up about six. After Eileen was seated in the truck, I handed her her walking sticks.

"Well," I said, "looks like we're finally in the soup together."

She laughed. "Soupmates. Reminds me of the day I said we should to open up shop together in downtown Oakland. Holing and Mallory. God, what a team—eh, Beth?"

Beth smiled. "Awesome." She started the engine and as they drove away, Eileen tossed me a jaunty wave.

WHEN I ARRIVED AT THE CLINIC later that morning, Jake and Winifred were in the supply room. Winifred was working in the filing cabinets, and Jake was sorting out his kit supplies. I don't think they were even aware I was there until I said to Jake, "I told you once I'd made up my mind what I was going to do about Luminex, I'd let you know."

They simultaneously stopped what they were doing and looked at me.

I said, "It has been a little over a month since your lawyer drew up the separation agreement, so I still have some time. Starting today, I'm going to document every deformed animal birth I know of in this valley. I'm going to ask—beg if I have to—owners of involved animals to give me signed, written statements. Your clients and mine."

Jake snapped his kit shut. "You'll make a lot of people angry."

Before I could reply, Winifred said tartly, "And it won't do you any good. People won't talk to you."

"Marilyn talked to me. Paul Milo talked to me. Arnold Brier's foreman talked to me. There'll be more."

Winifred closed her file drawer, hard.

Jake said, "You could get hurt, Nora."

"So could you."

MAKING CALLS AFTER THAT, I ASKED everyone whose animals I treated if their stock or pets had been affected or if they knew of anyone whose had, or whether they had suffered ill effects from Luminex themselves. I did the same thing at places Jake was in charge of.

Some of the large ranchers and dairy farmers were furious at what they perceived as an intrusion. One ordered me off his land, threatening, "You tell Jake if he can't take care of my animals like he always has, we'll get a vet over from Clarksville."

Some who brought their animals into the clinic for treatment marched right out of my examining room when I started asking questions.

Yet I had encouraging experiences to balance those.

One young high school botany student, whose zeal for plant life reminded me of Timothy's, took me to see a century plant that had been affected by the spraying. The spraying company stated ten miles was the maximum distance Luminex could be carried on winddrift. However, the century plant—twelve miles from the nearest spraying site—was flowering out of season. The young man pointed out immature new plants growing on the stocks of old ones instead of from normal seed set by the parent plant. He looked at me helplessly. "It's confused." After a moment, he went on, telling me that in order to document how far Luminex actually drifted on wind currents, I ought to have soil samples analyzed at escalating five-mile intervals from sprayed areas.

I took his advice and discovered toxic-laden Luminex had been carried as far as twenty-five miles.

A few days after that, a woman whose elderly Airedale was one of my favorite patients led me out to a small vegetable garden behind her house. Everything in it was dead. She said it had all died within two days of the April spraying. Having been through this during previous sprayings, she'd taken "before" and "after" pictures and saved the dated negatives, though she'd given up hope of anything ever being done.

Next, a poultry farmer called and asked me to come and see the netted enclosure where he was keeping chickens that had been born with paralyzed legs and wings. I told him about the number of similar incidents Marilyn's networking had turned up, and he said if I thought he could do some good by going to Washington, he'd buy a plane ticket tomorrow.

Exactly two weeks after my appointment with Dr. Kester, I called to ask about the results of her case count of miscarriages. The number was greater than she'd anticipated, and as I'd expected, the incidence was definitely higher in the spring.

"Would you be willing to ask those women if they would talk to me?" I asked, knowing that if she said yes, she would be putting herself at risk.

She did say yes, adding that she had recently learned about a laboratory in Sacramento that performed blood tests to assess the presence of certain chemicals. Maybe Luminex was one they could measure.

Then she gave me a list of general practitioners and obstetricians within a thirty-mile radius of Combsea and suggested I send a questionnaire inquiring whether they, too, had noticed a marked increase in miscarriages in the three-month period following the spraying, or an increase in children born with birth defects within nine months of the previous year's spraying.

I told her I'd send out the questionnaires that week. And as soon as I hung up, I dialed the number she'd given me for the laboratory in Sacramento. They affirmed that they could test for Luminex.

I spent the next night preparing and mailing my questionnaire to the doctors, asking them to respond as quickly as possible. Many didn't respond at all. But some wrote back acknowledging increases in miscarriages as well as in infants born with birth defects. I telephoned these and asked them if, like Dr. Kester, they would contact the women involved and inquire whether I might interview them.

Several said yes.

SOMEHOW I WASN'T SURPRISED when I saw the name of Arnold Brier's wife on one of the miscarriage lists. That spring day in the pasture at Briervale, I'd glimpsed the agony in her eyes and sensed it encompassed far more than the dying calf. Yet I *was* surprised she'd told her doctor she would see me.

I telephoned to ask when we might meet.

"Come to Briervale this week," she told me. "Arnold's in Sacramento for a few days."

I asked, "Would it be all right if I stop in around three tomorrow afternoon?"

"That would be fine."

Eileen called that night to find out what I'd been up to and to tell me what was going on at her end. She said she and the firm's computer consultant were putting in such long hours, he was thinking about renting an apartment in the building across the street from the law firm.

"And where and when do you sleep?" I wanted to know.

I could hear the grin in her voice. "Hell, I put a sleeper-sofa in my office weeks ago. Yesterday Rupert asked if I knew when I co-signed the lease on the townhouse that I was supposed to live there."

DRIVING TO BRIERVALE the next afternoon, the July heat seemed oppressive, but more than likely, it was my mood. Luminex was like a guerrilla foe. I'd met it once; now what I kept encountering were its effects. Talking to so many of its victims was making my anger increasingly difficult to control. So I was glad Arnold Brier was away. Every time we came within speaking distance, I lost control.

On my first visit, after passing under a wooden arch with "Briervale" carved across it, I'd taken the left turn Winifred had told me would lead to the barns and pastures. This time, following Celia's instructions, I turned to the right. The road wound to a manicured expanse of green lawn and a sprawling brick ranchhouse graced by a wide, shaded veranda. A paved parking area as big as a tennis court fronted a three-car garage.

Celia Brier was standing by the veranda steps and as soon as she saw me, hurried to meet me. I noticed again the almost haunted look in her eyes as she said, "I tried to reach you to tell you not to come, but Winifred said you didn't answer her page."

I frowned. "When did you call?"

"Within the past hour."

It didn't surprise me that Winifred hadn't paged me. She knew I wasn't seeing Celia on clinic business, and as far as Winifred was concerned, the more flack I got, the better.

"What did you want to tell me?"

"Arnold came home a little while ago. His meetings in Sacramento didn't take as long as he thought. Perhaps we should—"

Before she could finish, her husband came around the corner of the house. When he saw me, he stopped short between his wife and me. It was a complex moment. I wanted to move to one side to keep Celia in my view yet I felt doing that would be a concession to him—so I stayed put.

He asked sharply, "What are *you* doing here?"

"I came to talk to Mrs. Brier."

He looked at his wife. "You invited her?"

"Yes."

"What for?"

I could tell from her worried expression Celia was searching for a conciliatory answer.

I intervened. "I asked Mrs. Brier if she would talk to me about her miscarriages."

"I don't believe this. My wife's miscarriages are none of your business!"

"They are if they're related to Luminex," I said quietly, determined not to lose my temper.

"Related to—" He shook his head as if I were a hornet buzzing around his ears. "They don't have a damn thing to do with Luminex, and I resent the hell out of you trying to propagandize the fact that my wife isn't strong enough to carry a child to term."

"God, have you even read the toxicity reports on Luminex? Are women all over this valley 'not strong enough'? Is that what you tell yourself so you can keep on spraying?"

A tiny flame lit in his gray eyes, and at the same moment I heard Celia's soft intake of breath. Arnold Brier's hands came up in what I took to be a striking motion, and I flinched. Either I was wrong or he transformed it with lightning speed by leaning down and flicking a speck of dust off his boot. When he straightened up again, his face had no expression and neither did his voice. "You leave now, miss, and don't come back."

Celia quickly took a step forward. "I'll walk you to your car, doctor."

Understanding she was consenting to her husband's demand for me to leave, but also making it possible for us to have a few moments alone, I sensed her life was riddled with such compromises—keeping the peace while plotting a secret, stubborn course of her own.

As we walked down the veranda steps and across the green lawn to the parking area, Celia murmured, "Arnold grew up in hard times. He honestly believes what he's doing is right."

I was too furious to be diplomatic. "Right, hell," I said. "He believes in profit. He's blind to everything else."

She was silent.

I said, "That was rude. I'm sorry."

"He does care for me, doctor," she murmured, glancing at me quickly and then away.

I sighed. "Are you still willing to answer some questions?"

"I'll try."

"When did you miscarry?"

"This past May, and two years ago, in April."

"Were you directly exposed to Luminex either time?"

She said it was possible; it was her habit to go horseback riding early in the morning, and each year she'd been able to tell when the spraying had happened by the silence along the bridle paths. "It's curious. There isn't any insect noise after the spraying. You don't even know you've been hearing it until it isn't there any more."

"Didn't you have the spraying schedule?"

"Arnold keeps it in his desk. I asked him for it once, and he said I didn't have to worry, that he'd checked the winddrift report and the spraying didn't come anywhere near the bridle paths."

"Will you sign a statement that your miscarriages are connected with exposure to Luminex?"

"I don't know for certain that they are."

"Do you believe they are?"

She met my eyes. "I do."

"Will you submit to a blood test to determine whether your tissue contains Luminex?"

She didn't answer directly. "Would Arnold have to know?"

"He might some day."

She paused, giving a little shake of her shoulders. "All right."

I wrote down the name of the laboratory in Sacramento and gave it to her.

Reaching into the pocket of her yellow skirt, she took out a folded piece of paper and handed it to me.

I read the name, Priscilla Tyler, and a phone number.

"You should talk to Priscilla," Celia said. "She had a baby boy last December." When her eyes met mine again, they had the same expression I'd seen in them last spring.

"Is something wrong with her baby?"

Celia nodded.

"She's willing to talk to me?"

"Yes."

I put the piece of paper in my pocket and opened the door of the Jeep.

"Doctor—"

I waited.

"Sometimes I'm grateful my babies didn't live. I'm stronger than Arnold thinks I am, but I don't believe I could go through what Priscilla's facing."

She turned and walked back toward the house. Arnold was waiting for her on the veranda.

AS SOON AS I GOT BACK to the clinic, I called Priscilla Tyler and made an appointment to talk to her the next day. She, her husband, John, and infant son, Scott, lived in a frame house off the highway, between Combsea and Clarksville.

Priscilla invited me into a small, immaculate kitchen where she offered me coffee at an oak table that reminded me of Nell's. She told me her husband worked for the Forest Service, and one of his jobs was to hose out Luminex storage cans after they were emptied. On the evening of a day he had hosed out several Luminex cans, John had come home and played briefly with his son before he went to take his usual before-dinner shower. A few hours later, Scott was critically ill.

The emergency room doctor recognized Scott's pinpoint pupils, respiratory distress, and convulsions as possible symptoms of toxic poisoning. Blood tests confirmed the diagnosis. The baby had apparently absorbed Luminex residue through his skin while John was playing with him. Though not toxic enough to produce observable symptoms in an adult, the chemical could derange the nervous system of a two-month-old.

Priscilla told me Scott, now seven months old, was their only child. He lay near us in a crib by the kitchen window, and Priscilla invited me to come close to see him. "Hi, Scott," I whispered. The baby had blue eyes, a small pugged nose, soft gold hair crowning his head, and perfect tiny hands and feet.

Priscilla explained she didn't ever leave him alone but instead carried him with her from room to room while she moved about the house.

As we sat talking, she got up every few minutes to go look at him.

I could tell by the expression on her face when he was convulsing, although he made no sound. I went to stand beside her. A second later, my own hands and stomach constricted in rhythm with Scott's seizures as his body clenched and unclenched over and over.

Afterward, sitting at the table, if Priscilla looked directly at me, I could be still because her eyes transfixed me. When she wasn't looking at me, some part of my body kept moving—a foot tapping, or my fingers bending, unbending.

She said, "The doctors say he feels no pain when it happens. But how can they be sure?"

"I don't know."

"He probably won't live very long. How can he?"

I was silent.

"What's worse, I don't know if he should live. For him to go on like this seems like keeping a child in hell."

"I understand," I said, remembering Celia's remark about being grateful her babies didn't live.

Trying to sound professional then, I explained to Priscilla that signing a statement against Luminex could set in motion a chain of risks: John could lose his job with the Forest Service, and his medical benefits, which were paying for Scott's care, would then be jeopardized.

She said, "I know. I've thought about those things. But if we don't sign, we're saying what's happened is all right. I couldn't live with that."

THAT NIGHT, I TRIED to lose myself in typing material to send to Eileen—which was how I spent most evenings now. The firm was continuing to support her work on the Luminex case, although the senior counsel had warned her she was going to be one in a long line filing for an administrative-law hearing. It could be a year, maybe two, before her turn came up in court, and much, much longer before the matter was ruled on.

The firm's science consultants cautioned her not to expect to find any easily defensible, cause-and-effect equations in the material Marilyn, the other women, and I were sending. They said the human body was a constantly changing mosaic of hundreds of interrelated systems, and any argument which proposed regulating substances suspected of causing but not known to cause injury offered chemical company lawyers a target as big as a brontosaurus. Yet they also reinforced what she had said: the more concentrated the population she was dealing with, the more effective her arguments would be.

Unable to sleep after I finally went to bed, I got up and started writing something I sensed would take me a while to finish.

During the next several nights, sitting at my desk long after midnight, I put down my feelings about my own and Celia Brier's and other women's miscarriages, the livestock deaths and deformities I had witnessed, and Marilyn's moratorium. I wrote about Priscilla Tyler and her son, Scott, and I asked the question, Should life continue to be conceived and then exposed to substances that destroy or deform it?

When I'd finished, I realized I had written a plea. I didn't know what to do with it except send it to Eileen.

She called the day she got it. "Nora, reading that made me realize it's time for you to go to another town meeting. When's the next one?"

"It's always the last Wednesday of the month."

"That gives us some time."

" 'Us'?"

"I'm working on the final version of my petition for a hearing. I want to test it in front of the toughest audience I can find, and those council members in Combsea ought to fill the bill. I'll fly out the day before, but we'll keep my appearance at the meeting a surprise. However, people all over the valley should know ahead of time you're going to be there and what you're going to talk about. Can you get the word out?"

I didn't even stop to think. "Yes."

But after I hung up, I sat by the phone wondering how I was going to do what she'd asked. The more I thought about it, the surer I was that there wasn't a better person to help me than my landlord. If he would.

The next afternoon, I told Henry what I was doing and what I needed. I wanted him to deliver the mail one more time.

He said, "You could be opening up a real hornet's nest."

"I know. And I don't want to get you in any trouble."

"Hell," he said, "I'm too old to worry about that. Besides, this damn Luminex thing has stuck in people's craws for a long time. Just 'cause they keep silence doesn't mean they aren't hurting." Then his face kind of lit up. "I still know every road and mailbox in the county. You just give me your letters and the use of your jeep." That Saturday and Sunday, he drove around the valley, putting a copy of what I'd written in every mailbox on his old mail route.

As I expected, there was an almost immediate backlash: people calling to say they would not bring their animals to the clinic as long as I was there; accusatory phone calls and letters—some anonymous, some not; marauders vandalizing my house and land. One morning while I was taking a shower, somebody threw a rock through my kitchen window. I grabbed my bathrobe and ran outside to do battle, but of course whoever it had been was gone, or else hiding. Someone else—and the irrationality of the act enraged and frightened me— inflicted several deep axe cuts on a pine tree in the grove.

Then one evening I came home to find Will Jenkins standing in my driveway. The door to my house was open, hanging crookedly as if someone had forced it open. Remembering the morning Will and I had freed the wolf, the thought that he could become my enemy and invade my house—a personal violation akin, in my mind, to rape— filled me with a sense of mingled dread and futility.

"What are you doing here, Will?"

His eyes met mine, and then he looked away. "I heard some of the guys at school were going to come out here and break into your house."

I glanced at my door. "I gather they succeeded."

"They were already inside by the time I got here. I peeled some rubber in your driveway, honked my horn, told them somebody was coming and they were going to get caught. They took off."

I started toward my house, then turned. "Thank you for stopping them. Have you been inside?"

He shook his head.

I walked up the steps and into the house. All my books were on the floor. A lamp was turned over. Some black sticky stuff that looked like axle grease was smeared on my bathroom mirror. I'd left a few dishes in the kitchen sink, and they were broken. Suddenly I was shaking all over. I sat down on a kitchen chair and tried to make the trembling stop.

I heard Will come up onto the porch and say, "I think I can fix your door. If you want me to."

I couldn't even answer.

"I'll need a hammer and screwdriver."

The kitchen chair I was sitting on was next to the tool drawer. I opened it and took out the tools. Holding them brought back some common sense reality. The trembling eased. I got up and gave the tools to Will.

While he was fixing the door, I put my books back on the shelves, washed the bathroom mirror, and started cleaning up the broken dishes in the kitchen.

When Will called out that he had finished, I asked if he wanted a cup of coffee or a cold drink. His "No" was voiced in such an angry tone, I went into the living room. He was standing by the door that now hung straight. He glared at me. "Don't think I'm on your side just because I fixed your door. What you're doing is making it hard for everybody in this valley." Then he left.

I listened to him get into his truck and drive away, then slowly finished putting the broken dishes in the garbage. Damned if I was going to cry.

Somehow Paul Milo heard what happened at my house, and he started dropping by in the evenings to make certain I was all right, telling me to call him any time I needed help. Then Zelda or Ray began bringing hot cinnamon rolls over when they saw me drive into the clinic parking lot in the mornings. Mavis Wilson left a honeycomb on my doorstep. Women I didn't know wrote supportive letters. New clients started seeking out the clinic, driving what would normally be impractical distances from towns at the far end of the valley. People with whom I interacted on a regular basis—the mechanic who serviced my Jeep, the roofer who periodically mended the cabin roof—went out of their way to be helpful.

The week before the town meeting, Dr. Kester called to tell me she and a few colleagues she lunched with regularly had begun noticing a marked decrease in the number of pregnancies among their patients, and an increase in birth control consultations. "Nothing earthshaking," she said. "Maybe it's related to what you're doing and maybe not."

She went on, "My colleagues are inclined to attribute what's happening to coincidence, but they're still intrigued enough to compile some figures comparing this year to previous ones. We agreed next April, May, and June, the peak months for confirmed pregnancies, should provide the best test. So come next spring, I'll have some more statistics for you."

Since I hadn't told her—or anyone else—about my leaving the clinic, I had to say, "I may not be in Combsea then. But I can tell you where to send the information once you get it." And I gave her the name and address of Eileen's law firm.

"You're leaving Combsea, Nora?"

"I'm leaving the clinic," I said. "I'll have to find another position. I'm not sure where that will be."

She said, "Then I'll send the information to Eileen. But that doesn't mean I'm accepting your leaving. No way."

DIRECTIONS

"If we don't change our direction,

we will end up where we are heading."

Chinese Proverb

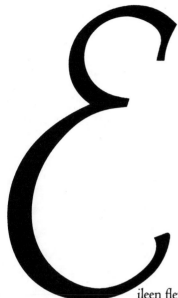ileen flew into Sacramento the Tuesday before the town meeting, and Beth brought her from the airport. I could see she was physically exhausted when she reached my house, but her eyes were crackling with excitement.

After dinner, as we relaxed in the living room, she said, "I could tell from the material you sent how hard you've been working. But Nora, you have circles under your eyes a raccoon would envy, and you've lost weight. Are you okay?"

I had to smile at the shoe being on the other foot. "Sure. Dreading tomorrow night, of course, but otherwise ..." I shrugged.

"You're going to be fine. You're tough, feisty, sharp-eyed, and scared —in short, a typical activist. Believe me, I know one when I see one."

"Yes, well, I'll just be glad when it's over."

Eileen looked at me. "It's never over." Then she asked what I was planning to say.

I wasn't comfortable yet with my speech. In fact, I was beginning to think I'd poured too much into the letter Henry had delivered, because nothing I'd written since had come up to that. I told Eileen I was still working on it.

We were silent for a moment. Then she said, "The woman in Three Rivers, Oregon, died."

I sat staring blankly at my hands.

She sighed. "And another in Montana."

"Are you going to mention that tomorrow night?"

"I thought I would."

"What else?"

She summarized it, and I listened intently. Then she said, "You're speaking first, of course. After you've finished and it's my turn, I want you to watch the council members and the people in the audience. I'll need to know how they react to what I say."

We were about ready to call it a night when I heard someone pull into the driveway. It was Paul. When I opened the door, he said, "I know it's late. I'm not coming in. I was passing by and wanted to make sure you're okay. And to tell you I'll be leading the cheering section tomorrow night."

I smiled. "Thanks, Paul. But come in for a minute at least. I want you to meet someone."

He stepped into the house, and Eileen got up from the couch and came forward. As he took her fragile hand in his, she smiled and said, "About time we met. I've heard good things."

"Well," he said, "they're all true."

Eileen chuckled.

She looked small standing next to Paul. But then, she always looked small—until she went into action.

I WENT THROUGH THE NEXT DAY at the clinic on automatic pilot, thankful I didn't have an emergency; I was hoarding energy for the meeting.

I think Jake and Winifred were surprised I'd even showed up for work. Winifred behaved as if I were invisible—whisking past me in the hallway, ushering clients briskly into my examining room without a word. And she'd arranged a schedule for Jake that kept him out of the clinic the entire day.

When I got home, Eileen was almost ready. She'd put on a severely tailored dark green suit ("forest green," she said) and was vigorously brushing her hair. When she put down the hairbrush and asked, "How do I look?" those great eyes were like moving circles of energy. I murmured, "Fine. God, you look fine."

Then I hurried to get ready myself, choosing a conservative paisley blouse and flannel skirt.

When I walked out into the living room, Eileen studied me for a moment then said, "Look at these outfits. You'd think we were going to church." A little toss of her head. "Well, maybe we are. I hope God's listening."

Though the council meeting probably wouldn't get under way until seven-thirty, we left my house an hour early—wanting to find seats near the front so Eileen wouldn't have far to go on her walking sticks when it was her turn to speak. To my surprise, about two dozen people were milling around the auditorium when we walked in. And then I remembered what Henry had said.

"You want to bet it's a sellout?" Eileen whispered.

We sat down and watched the auditorium fill up. By 7 p.m., all the metal chairs had been taken, and people were standing along either side of the room and in the back.

I was astonished at the size of the crowd, but Eileen just grinned. She sat forward like a thoroughbred in the starting gate at the Derby.

Two harried-looking high school students who had been summoned apparently on short notice came running up the center aisle, scurried around to the back of the stage, brought out a public address system, and began setting it up. In the back of the auditorium, there was a mobile TV unit from the station in Clarksville and a couple of reporters—at least I guessed they were reporters—with cameras and notebooks. Scanning the audience, I glimpsed Marilyn's face somewhere near the middle of the auditorium and Dr. Kester far in the back. A couple of rows behind Dr. Kester, I was surprised to see Will Jenkins about four seats down from Mavis Wilson. Priscilla Tyler was standing on the side next to a man I assumed was her husband, and he was holding Scott. Henry Mahler and Paul Milo were sitting together in the middle of the fourth row. Paul grinned and raised his fingers in a victory sign.

Then I saw Jake enter the auditorium. He stood among the people in the back, but he still seemed isolated.

When Arnold Brier took his seat on stage, he didn't look at me, and I didn't look at him. I hadn't seen Celia.

Shortly before seven-thirty, the council chairman picked up the microphone that had been placed on the table only moments before and announced he was going to dispense with the reading of the minutes and move immediately to matters of new business. Looking directly at me, he said, "Dr. Holing, I understand you wish to speak."

I stood up slowly, alarmed. I was still uncomfortable with my speech and realized I'd been counting on the reading of the minutes as a final priming time. If anyone had asked me if I was ready, I would have said, No! My hands were shaking. In confusion, I shoved my notes in my pocket and looked at the short flight of steps going up to the stage. They were fairly steep, and not wide enough to accommodate Eileen's walking sticks. Knowing she was planning to speak right after me, I moved to the empty space between the stage and the first row of seats and said, "If you'll pass the microphone down, I'll speak from here."

The chairman said, "I think it would be best if you came up here on stage and used the microphone."

But immediately people in the back of the auditorium called out, "Can't hear you." "Louder!"

I held out my hand for the microphone.

With a grimace—but he had to get this over with—the chairman got up and handed down the microphone.

It was a small victory, but it helped.

Then I heard Eileen murmur, "Go get 'em, Nora," and my clenched stomach relaxed a little more.

I'd never spoken into a microphone. Holding it, looking out at the audience, I focused briefly on Marilyn because her presence gave me courage.

Then I looked at Priscilla Tyler, and suddenly I was hearing her words—"If we are silent, we are saying what's happened is all right."

That wasn't what I'd planned to start with, but those were the first words I spoke into the microphone. Then I asked if anyone in the audience had ever talked to Priscilla or her husband, John, about what had happened to their son.

And I kept on asking questions:

How much did they really know about what was sprayed on their forests and rangeland, and then drifted on the wind over them?

Did they have any idea how many women in the valley aborted every spring? Or how many children's minds and bodies had been affected because their mothers had been exposed to the spraying?

How many of them had seen Marilyn O'Hare's foals the year her mares were exposed to Luminex?

Did they know what it was like to midwife a deformed animal, then administer death serum and hold that creature until its heart stopped beating?

And I asked how they could allow themselves and their loved ones and their children and this valley to be placed at such risk.

Then, though it seemed as if I'd just begun, the clock on the auditorium wall made me realize I'd been talking for almost half an hour . . . and I stopped.

I stood staring out at the faces until the chairman inquired coolly if I had finished. I answered, "Yes."

Eileen raised her hand immediately and asked for the floor. Before the chairman could respond, Arnold Brier leaned toward him, whispering urgently.

Eileen got up. I gave the microphone to her, then walked to the side of the room where I could watch the audience. A couple of people shifted to make room for me. I whispered, "Thanks," and smiled for the first time that evening.

Eileen leaned against the edge of the stage holding her walking sticks in one hand and the microphone in the other.

Arnold Brier finished his conversation with the chairman, who then turned to address the audience. But whatever he was about to say, he couldn't, because Eileen was already speaking. "Ladies and gentlemen, my name is Eileen Mallory. I am an attorney with a public-interest law firm in Washington, D.C. Over the past several months, I have been investigating Luminex, and I came here tonight to tell you some of the things I found out." The way her voice filled the auditorium I doubted she even needed a microphone.

The chairman broke in sternly. "Ms. Mallory, you have not been given the floor."

"I beg your pardon," Eileen said. "I asked to be recognized. When you didn't respond, I assumed I had the floor. What I have to say is directly related to the topic under discussion. May I go on?" She was holding the microphone so the audience could hear her, but not the chairman's soft reply.

"We have finished with the topic under discussion."

Eileen frowned. "I didn't hear you ask for comment from the other council members."

The chairman asked quickly, "Further comment, anyone?"

There was none.

But the audience was growing impatient.

"Let the lady talk!" someone shouted.

Another called out, "We want to hear what she has to say!"

Eileen said loudly, "Do I have the floor?"

With a helpless look at Arnold Brier, the chairman nodded.

Eileen turned back to her audience, her eyes moving down the rows, holding on one face, then another. Suddenly I understood why she loved being in court. She was a performer, and she'd already begun to work this room, too. Speaking as easily as if she were engaging the people there in conversation, she said, "During the referendum movement three years ago, I understand you were told if the spraying were stopped, logging trees would cost more. So would railroad transportation and maintaining electricity and telephone service. And raising cattle. Therefore, profits would have to be cut, and many of you would lose your jobs."

She paused. "In other words, you were threatened."

Arnold Brier abruptly shifted his position and his chair leg scraped on the wooden floor, but nobody paid any attention. They were listening to Eileen.

"People often give power to threats that don't really have power," she continued. "Luminex, for instance. It's not the equivalent of an earth-quake or a tornado. Its harm doesn't come from uncontrollable forces. Luminex is a chemical made by human beings and controlled by them.

"Yet when you think about the spraying, I don't think you see human beings controlling it. Instead you see railroads and lumber and utility and chemical companies. And that turns your feeling of being threatened into fear."

Will Jenkins was hunched over, elbows on his knees, chin in his hands, frowning intently as he listened.

"But I bet a lot of you ask yourselves, Why would chemical companies put a harmful substance on the market in the first place?

"I've heard one of their answers. They say they're achieving the greatest good for the greatest number. Which translates as: more people benefit from the killing of noxious weeds than are harmed by the illness or death of babies or animals or wildlife." She waited a moment. The whirring sound made by the TV unit amplified the silence. Her silence. She had them.

"Think about it," she said. "On one hand, thanks to Luminex, you have acres of weed-free rangeland and a bigger yield of loggable trees than you would have had otherwise. On the other hand, women who would have given birth to babies, haven't; Marilyn O'Hare's horses are barren; and Scott Tyler has uncontrollable seizures."

I glanced at the Tylers. Priscilla held her head high. Her husband had Scott clasped against his chest.

Eileen went on, "Another answer chemical companies give relates to their ability to control the toxicity of what they manufacture. They say for the good of the economy and their consumers, they must operate under a market equation, which means in order to stay in business, they must make money. Well, that's true. But believe me, they're making money.

"In many instances, they could have reduced toxicity by changing manufacturing processes, only that cuts into profits. And for some chemical companies, profit weighs far more heavily than individual pain."

Shifting her posture, Eileen went on, "I want to tell you now about a woman who lived in a town in Montana, a place pretty much like

Combsea. That town was sprayed each spring with Luminex. This woman had three miscarriages. She carried her last fetus almost to term. In her eighth month, her doctor couldn't feel her baby's head. He said they would have to induce birth, which they did. The baby—a boy—was perfect from his toes to his eyebrows, but that's where his body ended. His head was like an empty bowl covered by thin transparent skin. There was nothing inside. He didn't have a brain. That woman didn't want to go on living, and she didn't. She left a note giving permission to use her body in any way that might help. Recently, her doctor informed me that a sample of her body fat carried what they call a 'body burden' of Luminex far above the recognized 'safe' level."

I looked slowly around the room and certain women's faces held my gaze. One had her knuckles pressed tightly against her lips; another was rocking slowly in her chair. Up on stage, the woman next to Mrs. Mason was utterly still.

" 'Body burden' is a term chemical company scientists came up with because they know about the unpredictability of human response; they know that some people build up heavier 'body burdens' of chemicals than others. I'll read you a statement by one of NUMAR Chemical's laboratory chemists who acknowledged, and I quote, 'We are going to have to accept that random individuals might be sacrificed along the way by the use of Luminex.' "

Eileen's hand clenched her walking stick. "Who are these 'random individuals'? Was the woman in Montana one? Is Priscilla Tyler? How about her son, Scott? Are the women in this valley who aborted also 'random individuals'? If so, the dead fetuses were probably the most 'random individuals' of all."

I glanced quickly around the room for Jake. Either he'd moved where I couldn't see him—or he'd left.

Eileen continued, "The truth is, we are *all* random individuals with varying degrees of sensitivity to chemicals, and if a widely sold product poisons one person in five hundred, this means twenty thousand out of ten million will also be poisoned. And the marketing of chemical products that can do harm becomes an experiment with 'random individuals' serving as test animals."

She leaned toward them. "Please think about this: Chemical manufacturers cannot legally test their products on human beings because it's against the law. They used to be able to test them on prison populations—but not any more. They do test them on laboratory animals but often minimize or ignore the results of those tests, claiming that animal tests are not really applicable to people. For example, they say dosages that produce liver cancer in rats cannot be counted on to produce liver cancer in human beings. That's their terminology: 'counted on.' So, in a very real sense, by marketing substances with foreknowledge of their potential to do harm, they do test them on human beings—their consumers. In other words, they test them on you.

"Now listen to me. If you're exposed to a substance that can harm you and you haven't consented to that exposure, that makes you a victim, and you have the right and the responsibility to fight back."

A man in the back of the room spoke up. "Lady, how the hell do we know if stuff can harm us? We don't have time to check out every goddamn thing they throw at us."

"By yourself, no. Working together, yes."

The man shook his head, and she said, "I know. You should be able to rely on the federal agencies responsible for registering chemical substances put on the market. But you can't. Registration procedures are murky. The laboratories that test some chemical companies' products are financially controlled by those same companies. Registration rules keep changing. Some years they're stringent; other years they're lax. There are an incredible number of time-consuming appeal procedures that chemical companies can use to keep their products on the market if their registrations are suspended or canceled."

Another man stood up. "Then how can we find out?"

Eileen replied, "Data exists for every chemical on the market. Sometimes you have to fight for access to it. If you do, you can get it—under the Freedom-of-Information Act.

"You'll find out that laboratory tests performed on animals often forecast the potential for harm to people. You'll also find out about the illnesses chemical plant workers suffer. However, plant spokespeople say other factors are involved; through constant exposure, a worker can build up a 'body burden' of a toxic chemical much greater than someone who is only occasionally exposed. And, they say, companies can devise ways to protect their workers. Maybe they can, but many don't.

"The illnesses field workers suffer are similar. Literally thousands of agricultural workers have been poisoned harvesting food crops that have been sprayed with chemicals."

A young woman sitting in the middle of the room said, "I have a cousin in Paso Robles that happened to."

"Is your cousin okay now?" Eileen asked.

"He can work some days," the woman said.

" 'Some days.' " Eileen looked at the crowd. "During the referendum movement, when some of you questioned whether or not toxic chemicals should be sprayed on your valley, you were told the risks were too miniscule to worry about, that Luminex contained mere *trace* amounts of harmful molecules, and these were well below human tolerance levels.

"You were also told that chemical manufacturers were exploring new frontiers of science to benefit humankind; and it would be naive to expect them to stop producing widely used, highly beneficial chemical substances because test results showed certain lab animals were affected by them.

"As a clincher, they said if every toxic chemical were to disappear from the face of the earth tomorrow, the terrible things they were being accused of would continue to happen: people would still die of cancer; women would continue to abort; infants would be born with birth defects."

"And that's goddamn true!" Arnold Brier said loudly.

Eileen didn't look at him. "Now I'm asking: Are toxic chemicals a *possible* cause for people's afflictions? You bet they are, and in certain instances, a *verifiable* cause, because their effect on health is determined not by degree of exposure, but by individual sensitivity. For some people, there's no such thing as 'infinitesimal risk'; there is only 'risk.' That's true for fetuses, for newborns, for all susceptible mammals who nurse their young. And some of the risks being incurred today are through exposure to products whose complex effects over time will be so difficult to trace there will be no practical way to hold their manufacturers responsible.

"Is the gamble worth it?"

Several people muttered audible "no's," while others shook their heads.

"And what about those products and services if you're too sick to enjoy them? Or fruits and vegetables, if you're afraid to eat them because they've been sprayed; or water, if you can't drink it because it's contaminated; or fish, if they contain so many chemicals you don't dare cook them?

"Also, are your jobs any good if you're required to handle substances that make you or your children sick?"

"God, no," John Tyler whispered.

People looked at him and Scott, then quickly back at Eileen as she said, "All right. Let's assume you decide to raise a ruckus about Luminex and it's taken off the market, but the spraying goes on because another chemical takes its place. Will the new one do harm, too?" She waited a moment. "If it's another dangerous substance, yes!"

She put down the microphone—she didn't need it—and stood facing them on her walking sticks. "Today and tomorrow and the future are at risk. You must recognize—and make all companies who subject you to risk recognize—that there is a basic human commitment to preserving life that goes beyond cost-benefits.

"For god's sake, demand disclosure of risk about every substance you know you're exposed to without your consent. If they are poisonous, then you will know—and you must make chemical companies know that you will not allow those chemicals to be used.

"All I'm asking is for you to protect yourselves. Your lives are at stake. You are your own guardians."

Her eyes took in the whole room. "Thank you for listening."

Leaning heavily on her walking sticks, she moved back to her chair and sat down.

I knew she was in pain. But nobody else did.

DESTINATIONS

"I wake to sleep, and take my waking slow.
I feel my fate in what I cannot fear.
I learn by going where I have to go."

THEODORE ROETHKE

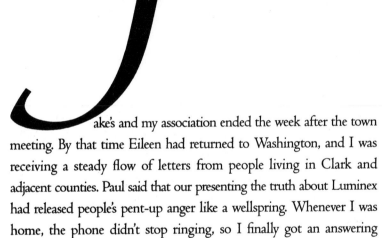

ake's and my association ended the week after the town meeting. By that time Eileen had returned to Washington, and I was receiving a steady flow of letters from people living in Clark and adjacent counties. Paul said that our presenting the truth about Luminex had released people's pent-up anger like a wellspring. Whenever I was home, the phone didn't stop ringing, so I finally got an answering machine.

For the next several months, I followed up on calls and letters and put that material in shape for Eileen. I drove all over the valley talking to people. But I missed working with animals, and each time I drove past the clinic, I felt a sense of loss.

Mavis said Winifred told her Jake probably wouldn't try to replace me, and even though work was what he needed, he was going to make himself sick if he didn't let up.

Henry tore up the rent checks I sent him and said he'd only take IOUs until things settled out. I'd been able to put some money aside every month I worked at the clinic, so that's what I lived on.

NELL CAME BACK FROM LONDON in late October, and I brought her up to date on everything that had happened.

I went to Santa Monica to spend Thanksgiving with her, and one night at the kitchen table, she said, "I came to this old house when I was about your age, Nora. It was one of my better decisions—that, and bringing you here."

I laughed. "I was a more dangerous decision than buying the house."

She smiled. "Speaking of houses, I was just wondering if Henry's cabin and land might be for sale."

This surprised me. "What if they were?"

"As I recall, there are two churches, two grocery stores, and two bars in Combsea. If Jake is going to practice solo, I would think there might be room for you to do the same."

I stared at her.

She said, "Give it some thought."

I don't think I slept at all that night. The next morning, I told Nell, "I'd have to talk to Jake first."

She nodded. "That's a good idea. Why don't you?"

IT WAS AN EARLY MORNING in mid-December when I drove to Jake's house. The sky was overcast and the air chilly. A light was on in his kitchen.

As I walked up onto the porch, Magruder started barking. I rang the bell and stood blowing on my hands until Jake opened the door.

I could tell he was surprised to see me but he didn't seem upset.

When I said, "Can we talk?" he asked if I wanted to come in.

"Okay."

Walking through the living room to the kitchen, I remembered the first time I'd done that. Now the living room looked cold and unused again. Faded images of who we had been were there for a moment, and the familiar anger and sadness started to surface. Entering the brightly lit kitchen, I pushed the feeling away.

Jake poured me a cup of coffee. "How've you been?"

"Busy."

"Yes, I've heard."

I said, "I expect things will quiet down after the spring spraying."

"Probably."

"I hear you're busy, too."

He nodded.

Then I started telling him what was on my mind. It didn't take long. It was clear there was more than enough work for two veterinarians in Combsea.

After I'd finished, he was quiet for several moments, staring into his coffee cup. Then he said, "You go ahead, Nora. It's all right by me."

"We could share emergency calls on holidays and weekends," I said. Thinking of Arnold Brier, I added, "Some, anyway."

He nodded. "That'd be good. Yes, I think it'll be okay."

"Thanks, Jake."

I saw something working in his face. I think the word that comes closest to describing it is—relief. He didn't want to be my enemy any more than I wanted to be his.

During the next few months while I continued organizing material for Eileen, I bought the cabin and built an addition twice the size of the original. The Holing Animal Clinic opened in mid-March. Nell came to see it and painted a mural in the reception room.

Marilyn was my first official client and Paul Milo, my second. He and I were seeing each other pretty regularly by then.

PEOPLE IN THE VALLEY did quiet down after the April spraying. There wasn't a lot they could do that they hadn't already done. But Marilyn, Dr. Kester, Henry Mahler, Priscilla and John Tyler, and Paul and I decided to establish a center to dispense information to other communities about verdicides and pesticides being used across the U.S., and Eileen immediately volunteered to be our legal assistant.

The cabin seemed the ideal place for it; in fact, in many ways, it already was "The Center." But we moved in more filing cabinets and tables, and as soon as we got set up, I put a big map on the wall and colored-coded it with pushpins. I used brown for areas sprayed with verdicides and herbicides, black for places where the abortion rate for human beings and other mammals was extremely high, and yellow for towns where the people had a high incidence of sarcoma and Hodgkins lymphoma, two cancers often associated with verdicides. Most of the time the brown, black, and yellow pins were all clustered together.

I described the map to Eileen, and she said her computer expert could put my data on a computerized grid map. But I said, "No, I need the sensation of sticking those pins in. It's my own personal voodoo."

In July, Dr. Kester reported the results of the study she and her colleagues had carried out. The number of pregnancies among their patients had significantly *de*creased.

I wrote about that in one of the Center's newsletters under the headline: "THERE'S A BETTER WAY TO CONTROL POPULATION THAN LUMINEX!"

I also mailed out hundreds of copies of an article Eileen sent me from the *American Journal of Public Health.* The article said numerous weeds and agricultural pests were developing resistance to verdicides and pesticides, so scientists were working around the clock developing new products. Chemical companies were especially optimistic about several genetically-engineered substances. However, a significant number of women agricultural workers exposed to these were giving birth to babies with missing and malformed arms and legs—similar to those associated with Thalidomide back in the sixties. "Thalidomide," the article said, "was the first substance to alert the public that chemicals producing little or no effect in a parent could profoundly influence the development of an unborn child."

An expert at the Centers for Disease Control in Atlanta stated, "The possible pesticide–limb reduction defect link is an intriguing possibility that might warrant further scrutiny."

Eileen had scrawled across the bottom: " 'Might'? My god, Nora, let's get back on the barricades!"

One evening after Paul and I had worked late on a mailing, Paul said it appeared to him there might be room for two generals now, and he asked me to marry him.

I said, "Between your ranch and my clinic and the Center, how would we ever find the time?"

"That's the easy part."

I said, "I'll think about it."

"How long?" His smile was weary but philosophical, and it got to me.

"Where would we live?" I asked. "Your place or mine?"

He glanced into the sleeping alcove. He didn't have to say anything. Filing cabinets were in there, too.

A few weeks later we were married, and I moved out to the ranch.

EILEEN'S PETITION FOR A HEARING on Luminex was eventually granted, but almost two years passed before she had her day in court.

During that time, the spraying continued.

The night before the hearing, Eileen called and told me she'd run her argument through the computer so many times to get it down to "pure pith," she pictured the machine's memory looking like the craters of the moon. "And mine, too. But Rupert tells me on my worst day, I can compete with most lawyers he sees on their best days."

"That doesn't sound like Rupert."

"Well, Nora, he's getting senile."

I lingered over breakfast the next morning picturing Eileen in the courtroom she'd described so often: the high ceilings, windowless lighting, rich-grained wood of the lectern and counsel tables, and the "bar" that spectators sat behind.

I remembered her saying once, "Kiddo, for me, it's like a cathedral."

She telephoned as soon as the hearing was over.

"How did it go?"

"Okay! Wheeling down the corridor, I overheard the Luminex counsel say he hoped I'd be on the next rocket to Mars—so I turned around and said, "Why? Do you spray up there, too?"

THE COURT'S DECISION REMAINED in abeyance while arguments continued to be presented on behalf of and in opposition to Luminex. Finally the arguments ended, and the court went into deliberation. We were all hoping for a decision before the end of the year, and rumor had it we were going to get one. But in early December—as the court was preparing to announce its findings—NUMAR Chemicals issued a public statement that they were abandoning production of Luminex. They told the press they were taking Luminex off the market because of public hysteria. "We don't really consider this a health and safety issue at all," their spokesman said. "It's a commercial issue."

Eileen's comment: "Bless the little fuckers' hearts."

A week later, even though travel was becoming increasingly difficult for her, Eileen announced she wanted to come west. She said, "Now that Luminex is off the market, my number-one priority is seeing the center." And with a mischievous edge to her voice, she added, "Besides, Rupert said he'd chauffeur me."

They flew in the night before New Year's Eve and got to the ranch-house just as dusk was edging into darkness. The moment I heard them pull into the driveway, I ran outside. Rupert was unfolding the wheelchair, and I leaned into the car and hugged Eileen before Rupert lifted her out. Then Paul was there, greeting Rupert and bending down, holding both Eileen's hands in his, exclaiming, "Damn, it's good to see you." Paul wheeled her into the house. He'd spent the afternoon preparing a great supper. Eileen was too exhausted to eat much, but she sampled everything. I was pleased to see Rupert did it justice.

Time hadn't marked him much. His green eyes were still startling against his dark skin, even more so now that his hair was turning light at the temples. This evening was the first occasion I'd had to witness the closeness that existed between him and Eileen. He was alert to her needs in a way that managed to be both tender and matter of fact.

After Rupert confessed he'd never been near ". . . an actual cow," Paul said he'd show him the ranch the next day—cows, pasture, and barn, plus his cache of hard cider.

Rupert perked up. "You mean spirits?"

I suspected they might ring in the New Year a bit early.

That night I lay awake thinking about Eileen. Even though she used the wheelchair all the time, if her hands were in spasm she had difficulty operating the electrical controls, and I knew how she must hate relying on others for mobility. Yet when I looked into her eyes— magnified now by the thick-lensed glasses she had to wear—I saw what I had always seen: undimmed energy.

The next morning, I was alone in the kitchen, so absorbed in thoughts about the day ahead, I didn't hear Rupert enter the room until he muttered, "How do you people get any sleep?"

I turned. "What do you mean?"

"Couple of times it sounded like someone was on the roof trying to get in."

"Probably a raccoon or a wood rat. Keep you awake?"

"Not that so much—but the screaming did."

I laughed. "A screech owl." When I handed him a cup of coffee, I asked, "Is Eileen up?"

"Yeah. But you know, it takes her a while." He moved to the window and stood looking out.

The December sun was shining, though there would be no warmth in it. Storm clouds were already forming on the horizon, and the mountain tops in the distance were tipped with snow.

Studying Rupert's profile, I was aware that the dislike we'd felt for each other during the old Berkeley years had melted away. I'd known for some time his being with Eileen was a good thing, and that he was stronger than I'd ever given him credit for.

I said softly, "I'm glad you're here."

He turned. "Yeah?"

"Yeah."

He sighed, walking toward me. "Well, I lose it sometimes. Last week, I was in the kitchen getting us some breakfast. She'd had a bad night. I was boiling eggs using one of those hourglass timers. Damn thing got to me. I picked it up and threw it against the wall, but it didn't break; so I stomped on it, ground it right into the linoleum."

His eyes met mine. On sudden impulse, I put my arms around him. His body was so stiff, I thought I might have made a mistake.

But then he held on to me, too, for a moment before he said, "I'll go check and see how she's doing."

I was busy putting breakfast on the table when I heard the two of them coming down the hallway and then a moment later, Paul walked in. Eileen had regained her appetite and ate a huge stack of pancakes. As we were all finishing a last cup of coffee, Rupert said to Paul, "The ladies look restless, so I guess it's time for me to go meet the cows."

Paul nodded. "And we'll check out the cider, too. Don't forget that."

"Fat chance," said Eileen as Rupert reached for his coat.

A few minutes later, he and Paul left the house. Eileen immediately wanted to know, "When can we go to the Center?"

I glanced out the window. Storm clouds had claimed more of the sky. I said, "We better leave now."

We bundled up, and I wheeled her out to the Jeep. Lifting her onto the passenger seat, I was startled at how light she was. As we drove along the valley road, rays of sun shone through the gathering clouds on pine and fir, and Eileen was quiet, taking it all in.

When we arrived, I stopped for a moment at the clinic to see how Beth was doing. Jake had agreed to be on call over the holiday weekend, and Beth was relaying all our emergency calls to him. While I checked the calls that had come in, Beth wheeled Eileen out to the reception room to see Nell's mural. Then we went over to the Center.

When we entered, the cabin was in its usual chaotic state—cartons of supplies on the floor, newspapers and magazines stacked up for scanning and clipping, piles of letters waiting to be answered.

Henry Mahler was there with his nine-year-old great-grandson. They were both stuffing copies of our latest newsletter into envelopes. About a dozen student volunteers were answering phones and opening and answering mail.

Eileen asked me where the young people had come from, and I told her Beth had put up flyers at the junior college and county agricultural school. Once the students started coming, they kept on.

However, I hadn't expected this many to be here today; after all, it was New Year's Eve.

Henry came forward to greet Eileen, then wheeled her around the room, introducing her to his great-grandson and the student volunteers. Some of them had heard about her and seemed a little awestruck, but Eileen chatted with them comfortably about their work and they soon relaxed.

I was watching her the same way Rupert did—alert for signs of fatigue. However, surrounded by all this activity, she looked almost jubilant, so it was hard to tell.

One young man left a table and went to stick a couple of new push-pins in the map; Eileen wheeled over, looking up at it. There were clusters of pins in every state. She took off her glasses and rubbed her eyes, then glanced at him and said, "It's going to be a long fight."

He nodded. "It sure is, ma'am."

"You planning to sign on for the duration?"

"You bet I am."

She smiled.

But I could see from the droop of her shoulders that she really was getting tired, so I said, "Maybe we should get back to the ranch."

She nodded, then went around the room, saying goodbye to every-one, shaking hands, and giving words of encouragement.

A light snow was falling as we left the cabin, and the wheels of her chair crunched on ground hardened from recent frosts. When we reached the Jeep, she said, "Three generations in there. You notice?"

I hadn't especially, because it was often like that.

"Damn, Nora, you really started something."

"*We* did."

She looked up.

"Holing and Mallory."

She chuckled. "That has a familiar ring to it."

Our eyes met.

"It's been some partnership," I said. "I wasn't sure we'd make it through the first month. Now look at us."

A few snowflakes had settled on her dark hair. As I lifted her up into the Jeep, she said, "I'm glad that young guy called me ma'am. Now I know kids his age see me as old, and that's something I didn't think I'd ever get to be." She grinned. "Hell, Nora, I'm old! Ain't it great?"

"Happy New Year," I answered.